"This w

Robert soothed as he began to work on the splinter in Miranda's finger. His eyelids were half-closed in concentration, giving him a slumberous look that sent a trickle of longing through her.

Miranda was so intent on watching him that she forgot about the tweezers—until they snagged a piece of skin.

"Ouch!" Miranda jerked her hand away and inadvertently knocked over the bag she'd brought home from the drugstore, spilling its contents onto the table.

"What are these?" Robert picked up the box of condoms.

Miranda flushed. "If you have to ask, I have a much bigger problem than I thought."

"Darling Miranda." Robert smiled, but the soothing timbre of his voice was gone.

"I wasn't going to make demands on you," she whispered as he pulled her closer.

"Feel free." His breath fanned her cheek. "Because I plan to make a few demands of my own...."

Popular **Judith McWilliams** continues
to delight her many fans with her
lighthearted, amusing stories. In *Sweet
Stuff* she mixes a madcap search for stolen
artwork with the heroine's concern over
her inability to form a successful
relationship. Judith, the author of eight
Temptation romances, and her family
make their home in Indiana.

Books by Judith McWilliams

Sweet Stuff
JUDITH MCWILLIAMS

Harlequin Books

TORONTO • NEW YORK • LONDON
AMSTERDAM • PARIS • SYDNEY • HAMBURG
STOCKHOLM • ATHENS • TOKYO • MILAN
MADRID • WARSAW • BUDAPEST • AUCKLAND

Published July 1992

ISBN 0-373-25504-7

SWEET STUFF

1

"MIRANDA?"

Miranda Sheffield jumped as her concentration broke; a thin stream of green icing spurted across the multitiered wedding cake.

"Jenny, I swear I'm going to tie a bell around your neck," Miranda snapped, the anger and frustration escaping from beneath the calm front she'd struggled to maintain for months.

"Sorry to invade your inner sanctum, but some lady is here to see you. She says she's your mother." Jenny sounded doubtful.

"I hope that's a compliment," said a slender woman wearing an elegantly cut teal-blue suit. She stepped around Jenny, her high heels clicking on the gray-tiled floor, walked briskly across the small kitchen and warmly embraced Miranda.

Miranda enthusiastically returned the hug. "Jenny, despite her absurdly youthful appearance, this really is my mother, Sarah Witmer. Mom, meet Jenny Rowinski, one of the most promising pastry chefs I've ever trained.

"Jenny, why don't you come back in a half an hour and help me add some leaves to the cake?" Miranda added, trying to make amends for her earlier shortness.

"Really? You mean it?" Jenny asked excitedly.

"Of course I mean it. The work you've been doing on the petits fours has been excellent. It's time you branched out into something a little more challenging."

Jenny practically skipped out. "She seems a nice young woman," Sarah observed.

"Uh-huh," Miranda absently agreed, much more interested in her mother's unexpected appearance. "I didn't even know you and David were in the country, let alone here in New York City."

"I tried to call you last night before I left Brussels, but I didn't get an answer at your apartment."

"I was here at the store until after midnight, working on a rush order." Miranda pulled her white chef's hat off her head and, tossing it onto the counter behind her, ran her fingers through her short, ash-blond curls.

"Sometimes it seems as if half the population of New York is getting married this fall. Usually the worst of the rush is over by now, but we're booked solid through early December," she added, trying to make it sound as if she had been working late because of scheduling pressures....

"That's because you're the best pastry chef in the whole city," Sarah declared loyally. "You don't just ice cakes. You create visual works of art." She gestured toward the towering cake with its cascade of intricately formed icing flowers. "It's no wonder that everyone wants to use your catering firm."

Hers and her ex-husband's. Miranda tensed. "Why don't you have a seat while I get us something to drink? I'm more than ready for a break," she suggested, hoping she'd managed to keep the strain out of her voice.

Miranda poured two cups of coffee, added cream and sugar to both and handed one to her mother. She perched on the edge of the stainless steel counter and took a cautious sip, watching her mother nervously play with the fingers of her black leather gloves. Miranda frowned, wondering what was wrong. Her mother's steel nerves in the face of disaster were legendary in diplomatic circles.

"Is something wrong with David?" Miranda probed when her mother made no attempt to break the uneasy silence.

"No." A fleeting smile briefly lifted Sarah's lips. "He's never been better. In fact, while it isn't public knowledge yet, he's going to be given the ambassadorship to Germany after the first of the year."

"Why, that's wonderful!" Miranda liked her stepfather, both for his own sake and because he'd made her mother happy.

"Is that why you're back in the country?" she went on. "So that he can consult with the State Department?"

"David isn't here. He couldn't get away and, since it was already too late . . ."

"Too late?" Miranda echoed.

"To help your Great-uncle Henry."

Miranda snorted. "It was too late the second he was born. That man has to be the original male chauvinist. He wouldn't accept help from a woman if he were up to his neck in quicksand and she was holding the only rope!"

Sarah sighed. "*Was* the original male chauvinist."

"Was?" Miranda repeated uncertainly.

"Henry died late last night."

"Died!"

"He had a massive heart attack and never regained consciousness. His lawyer called me, and I took the first flight over."

Miranda rubbed her forehead. It seemed as if a malevolent fate was determined to shatter her world beyond repair.

"Don't feel too badly," Sarah said. "Henry had a full, rich life and he didn't suffer in the end. He would have hated being an invalid."

Miranda managed a wry smile. "So would the nurse who would have had to have taken care of him. It's just that . . ." She sighed. "I know I haven't actually seen him in years, but I wrote to him and I knew he was there. If you know what I mean?"

"Yes." Sarah smiled sympathetically. "Henry loved you, you know. In fact, he left you the farm."

Miranda blinked. "I got the farm instead of Dad? That isn't going to sit any too well with my dear stepmother. She's a bit on the acquisitive side."

"Personally, I'd put it at greedy. But in this case she actually came out ahead. Henry left his investments in trust for the education of your half brothers."

Miranda frowned. "But why would Uncle Henry leave me the farm? He was always going on about how there had been Sheffields working that land since before the Revolution."

"According to the lawyer, Henry planned to sell the farm and leave you the proceeds, but changed his will when you wrote about your marriage breaking up."

"I would have thought that the stigma of yet another divorce in the family would have made him cut me out of his will altogether."

Sarah shook her head. "Henry never liked Jim. Come to that, neither did I."

"But you never said so. Not even when he demanded a divorce so that he could marry his girl-friend." She felt herself tense again at the humiliating memory.

"I never said anything while you were married because I didn't want to cause dissension, and four months ago you weren't ready to look at the situation objectively."

"I'm still not." Miranda grimaced self-deprecatingly. "I know it's silly. The divorce is final and he's already married his precious Brandy, but . . . I can't seem to let go. I feel . . ." She gestured. "Helpless. As if I'd lost control of my life. And to make matters worse, Jim now wants me to sell him my half of the business. He says it's impossible for us to work together."

"Are you going to?"

"Why the hell should I?" she exclaimed. "I gave him a divorce so that he could marry Brandy. Why should I give him the business, too? Why shouldn't I buy his half and he can start over somewhere else?"

"Because what made this place the second-largest catering firm in New York City is your talent. Without your reputation behind him, he'll be just one more catering firm. Jim may be an emotionally immature man, but he's not stupid. By the way, where is the rat? I didn't see him as I came through the offices."

"He's been doing most of his work at home. He says I make him uncomfortable," Miranda told her mother.

"Guilt." Sarah nodded sagely. "We are far crueler to the people we wrong than to the people who wrong us."

Miranda sighed. "You're probably right. You usually are."

"Trust me." Sarah gave her a loving smile that momentarily warmed Miranda's frozen heart. "Someday you'll send up paeans of thanksgiving that fate sent Brandy to rescue you from a dishwater-dull marriage."

"It wasn't all that bad," Miranda found herself protesting.

"Yes, it was. You just don't have anything to judge it against. Jim latched on to you when you were only eighteen, so you've never had a chance to learn about men."

"I know lots of men," Miranda objected.

"There's knowing and there's knowing. My advice to you is to start dating and find out what the opposite sex is all about. Just make sure that you're protected. There's a lot of nasty diseases running around out there."

Miranda stared at Sarah's earnest expression and her sense of humor, which she'd thought had died four months ago, stirred. "I don't believe this! My own mother is telling me to have an affair? What is the world coming to?"

"Honesty, for one," Sarah said emphatically. "You're not some impressionable teenager. You're a thirty-two-year-old woman who's never really explored what being a woman is all about."

"From where I'm standing, it's about pain and grief and rejection and being used. When are we leaving for Henry's funeral?" she inquired, determinedly changing the subject.

Sweet Stuff

"We aren't. The funeral isn't until day after tomorrow and I have to fly back to Brussels tonight. In fact, I asked the cab to wait for me."

"Tonight! But why on earth did you fly all that way if you can't stay for the funeral?"

Sarah's mouth tightened and for a second she looked every minute of her fifty-five years. "Because I had to get the pictures before someone else stumbled across them. Like that snoopy lawyer of Henry's."

"Pictures?" Miranda asked. "What kind of pictures could Uncle Henry possibly have that would necessitate a trip from Europe to collect them? Don't tell me the old boy had a penchant for naked women?"

"One of them was of a naked woman, but not the way you mean." Sarah grimaced. "Oh, blast Henry! I'd hoped that you'd never need to know about this, but now I'm going to have to pitchfork you right into the middle of it because I absolutely have to go home. The embassy is giving a mammoth reception next week, and I'm responsible for organizing it. I can't let David down. This is a very crucial time in his career, which is why we absolutely have to hush this up. Oh, Miranda, I'm so worried, I don't know what to do." Sarah's blue eyes filled with tears. "If David loses his ambassadorship because of me . . ."

"Nonsense." Miranda gave her mother an encouraging hug. "Everything will be fine. Just tell me what I need to do."

"Well . . . You see . . ."

"In fifty words or less," Miranda said firmly. "I can't fix it until I know what's broken."

"You really will help?"

"Of course." Besides, it would be nice to tackle a nonemotional problem that she had a reasonable chance of solving, she thought wistfully.

"Your Uncle Henry was an art thief," Sarah blurted out.

"Mom, Uncle Henry's idea of art was the picture on the calendar his life insurance company sent every year. Besides, where would he have found any art in the Adirondacks to steal, even if he'd have wanted to—which I find hard to believe? The man was a model of integrity."

"Oh, yes! But it was that uniquely masculine kind of integrity that makes a man protect women and children, but allows him to drop a bomb on them, provided their government is at war with his."

Miranda grimaced. "Point taken."

"It all happened while Henry was in Germany with the Allied occupation troops at the close of the Second World War. A lot of men brought home souvenirs and . . . well . . . Henry did, too."

"I take it he brought back pictures?"

Sarah nodded desperately. "A Rembrandt, a Rubens, a Da Vinci drawing . . ."

"*What!*"

"There were a couple more, but those were all I actually saw."

"Let me get this straight," Miranda asked incredulously. "My great-uncle looted a bunch of paintings from a German museum?"

"Yes."

"But how did he get them into the States?"

"He simply mailed them home. You have to remember that Europe was in a shambles, security was lax and, according to Henry, the prevailing sentiment was 'to the victor belonged the spoils.'"

"Good Lord, Mom! We have to find those paintings."

"Why do you think I flew all the way from Belgium?" Sarah said tiredly. "But unfortunately, it isn't going to be that easy. I already tried, but I couldn't search for them because that blasted lawyer installed a caretaker to make sure that the house wasn't vandalized before you could take possession. And to make matters worse, someone wants to buy the farm, which makes me wonder if Henry told anyone else about the pictures."

"It's possible, but not probable. Uncle Henry was a closemouthed sort of man. The wonder is that he told you."

"He didn't exactly. I was rummaging around in the bedroom one night during one of our visits, looking for extra blankets, when I stumbled across them in the back of the closet. When I asked Henry about them, he told me how he'd gotten them and swore me to secrecy. As if I'd want to spread it around that our family harbored an art thief," she said scathingly. "I never even told your father. I tell you, Miranda, I'm at my wit's end. Can you imagine what the press would make out of this if it ever gets out? I can see the headlines now. Prospective German Ambassador's Wife Implicated in Theft of Priceless German Art Treasures."

Miranda winced. "Much as I hate to admit it, you could well be right. A scandal like that wouldn't do David's career any good. But once we get the paintings, how do we return them?"

"Anonymously!" Sarah said vehemently. "We'll mail them to the German embassy in Washington from here. There's no way they could ever trace a package sent from New York City."

"Sounds reasonable. I can leave tomorrow after lunch," Miranda said, vaguely ashamed at the intense sense of relief she felt. Henry's funeral and her need to see to the estate she'd inherited gave her an unexceptionable excuse to escape what had become an intolerable situation, without seeming to cave in to Jim and Brandy's demands.

Sarah glanced at her watch and stood. "I have to run or I'll miss my return flight. You will call the minute you find them, won't you?"

"Certainly. You have a safe trip home and don't worry about a thing. I'll be on my way upstate by two tomorrow at the latest."

Unfortunately, Miranda's estimate turned out to be overly optimistic. By the middle of the following afternoon it was obvious that she wasn't going to be able to finish her work until late that evening. That meant she was going to have to leave before dawn the next day in order to arrive in time for Henry's funeral. It was unthinkable that he should go to his grave without at least one member of the family there to bid him Godspeed.

"Miranda!" Jenny burst into Miranda's private kitchen. "You'll never guess what Winnie down in the office just sent up!"

"It better not be another specialized order," Miranda said ominously. Winnie was a firm partisan of Brandy's and, since her friend's marriage to Jim, had been going out of her way to make Miranda's life difficult.

"No, it's a man." Jenny heaved a soulful sigh and added, "Unfortunately, it's you he wants to see."

"Me?" Miranda looked up in surprise. "Why?"

Jenny shrugged. "I don't know. He didn't say."

"You could ask."

Jenny frowned. "He isn't the kind of man you question."

"I'm never going to get this blasted cake finished," Miranda grumbled. "Where did you put him?"

"In your office, since it was empty. I just hope he stayed."

Not me, Miranda thought as she hurried down the hall. As far as she was concerned, he couldn't wander far enough. She simply didn't feel up to coping with anything else.

She pushed open the door to her office and stepped inside, blinking as the bright November sunlight pouring in through the large window, momentarily blinded her. She blinked again and her vision cleared, to reveal a man standing in front of the window in a waterfall of light. It gilded his dark brown hair with reddish sparks and added a golden patina to his sharply chiseled features.

Fascinated, her eyes slipped over the tailored perfection of his gray suit. She had no trouble understanding what Jenny had meant when she'd said he wasn't the kind of man one questioned. He exuded a confidence that must have been very daunting to the youthful Jenny. But not to her, Miranda encouraged herself. She was a mature, intelligent professional who took strange men in her stride. Even ones who looked as if they could have posed for Michelangelo's David.

"Miss Sheffield?"

"Yes, I'm Miranda Sheffield," she said after the faintest of pauses. She still wasn't used to being addressed by her maiden name. Reverting to it gave her some small measure of control over her life, she'd decided, badly shaken after the divorce. "And you are?" She offered her hand.

"Robert Deverill."

The sound of his voice was swallowed up in a surge of heat that engulfed her at the feel of his callused fingers closing over hers.

"Robert Deverill?" She started to block her reaction to him, then stopped. She wasn't married anymore. There was no disloyalty in allowing her body to respond to this man. Responding to attractive men was part of being single.

She willed her voice to briskness. "Your name sounds vaguely familiar, but . . ."

"Perhaps Henry mentioned me? He promised me that I could buy the farm when he retired. Unfortunately, he died first."

So this was the man her mother suspected of being on the trail of Henry's ill-gotten gains. Robert Deverill certainly didn't look like a thief. In fact, he looked as though he'd be right at home at one of her mother's diplomatic receptions.

"Miss Sheffield . . . It is Miss, isn't it?"

"I'm divorced." She tried to keep the pain she felt at the admission out of her voice.

The movement of his elegantly clad arm as he brushed away a piece of lint distracted her. Her eyes traveled over his arm, pausing to study the way the material molded his broad shoulders. Expensive material, she noted, wondering why a man who was wearing what was obviously a custom-tailored suit and handmade shoes wanted her uncle's property.

It was hard to believe that Robert Deverill's intentions were criminal, but why else could he want the farm? No one could possibly wrest a living from it. Not only that, but its location in the Adirondack Mountains made it hard to get to. Unless its very inaccessibility was the lure? Miranda stole a quick glance at Robert's face. Could it be that illegal drugs and not stolen art lay behind his interest in the property? Could he want the farm as a way station for the movement of drugs from Canada?

She eyed his face speculatively. His vaguely familiar face. She felt a strange frisson of déjà vu. As if she'd met him somewhere before. But where?

"Have you reached a conclusion yet?"

"What?" She scrambled to pick up the thread of the conversation.

"From your minute study of me. Or do you study all men like that?" He gave her a gleaming smile that made her stomach flip-flop.

"I was trying to figure out if you wanted the farm as a way station in a drug-running scheme," she said repressively, uncomfortable with his teasing. Her mother had been right, she thought grimly. She never had learned how to relate to the opposite sex on anything other than an intellectual level. But she could learn. She tilted her chin.

His hazel eyes gleamed greenly with sudden amusement, sending another surge of excitement through her.

"Do I really look like a drug dealer?" He seemed more curious than offended.

She shrugged. "How would I know? The only ones I've ever seen were on the evening news. Usually lying facedown in the street, covered with blood. One is not inclined to look too closely."

"I suppose not," he conceded. "But to put to rest all your imaginings, I am not into the drug scene. Not as a user or a supplier. I value my body far too much."

"I can understand that," Miranda murmured, then flushed when he laughed.

"Thank you," he said solemnly.

Miranda winced. Taking refuge in the impersonal subject of the farm, she said, "I will not sell Uncle Henry's land to you, and I don't have time to argue about it. I'm up to my ears in work."

"At least up to your neck." He brushed green icing off her chin.

Miranda held her ground with an effort; the fine hairs on her cheek had suddenly become electrified.

Robert frowned, suddenly serious. "What good is a neglected farm to you? If you sell it to me, you'll be able to look around for a better job."

Miranda stared at him, trying to decide if it was to her advantage to let him go on thinking that she merely worked here or to tell him that, far from needing money, as he seemed to think, she was very comfortably off.

"One where you didn't have to spend your days baking cakes," he added persuasively. "I'll even pay to have all of Henry's effects packed and shipped down here to you."

"In the first place, the cake was baked two days ago, and I didn't do it. I decorate them. I also don't need the money from the farm. I own half of this business," she said, deciding that the truth would be one less lie to keep track of. She had a depressing feeling that she was going to be chin deep in lies before this escapade was over.

"Has someone made you a better offer for the farm?"

"As the saying goes, read my lips. I am not going to sell the farm. Not to you. Not to anyone."

"But . . ."

"Because I intend to live there myself," she improvised.

"You intend to live on Henry's farm! By yourself?" The wicked gleam in his eyes made Miranda nervous, but she refused to retract her words. If he thought she intended to live there permanently, maybe he'd leave her alone long enough for her to locate the paintings.

"Yes, I intend to live there by myself," she reiterated. "I am very self-reliant."

"To say nothing of foolhardy."

"Come now, Mr. Deverill. Upstate New York is hardly on the edge of civilization."

"You'd better call me Robert, since we're going to be neighbors."

"We are?" she asked dubiously.

"Most assuredly." He gave her a smile that made her feel as if she'd missed something somewhere. "Since I'll be seeing you in the near future, we can continue our discussion then."

He was out of the door before Miranda could respond, although what she would have replied she didn't know. Robert Deverill's visit had given rise to more questions than answers. She didn't know why he wanted the farm. Nor why he seemed so familiar. And she didn't have the vaguest idea what he did to pay for the hand-tailored suits he obviously favored.

"Tell me it isn't true." Jenny's anguished voice came from the doorway.

"Considering the way my life has been going lately, I'd come down heavily on the side of yes," Miranda said wryly. "However, knowing the question would make it easier to be sure."

"You aren't really going to go live on some godforsaken farm upstate, are you?" Jenny wailed.

"Nothing has been decided yet. And what were you doing outside the door, eavesdropping?" Miranda asked.

"Well, the eavesdropping part was unintentional. You see, I finally figured out who he was. He's Robby Deverill, the tennis player. I saw him win Wimbledon when I was in high school. He had the most awesome backhand," Jenny said reverently.

"So that's why his face was familiar," Miranda said slowly. "He announced his retirement when I was in France about five years ago, and his name and picture were in all the papers. From what I remember, he was pretty good."

"In a class all by himself," Jenny said enthusiastically.

"So why'd he retire?" Miranda asked curiously. "He couldn't have been that old."

"Thirty-three," Jenny supplied, "but that's pretty old for a tennis player. Besides, there wasn't any reason for him to hang on. He'd already won everything worth winning at least twice, and according to the press, he was one of the smart ones. He invested his earnings."

"But that makes no sense," Miranda said in confusion.

"It makes a lot more sense than blowing it all on a wild life-style, like so many sports figures do. Not that he needed the money. I read somewhere that he inherited tons of money from his mother's family. She was

the daughter of some big German industrialist. Deverill's father met her when he was a visiting professor
at the University of Hamburg."

"German?" Miranda felt a chill of foreboding.

"Uh-huh. He has dual citizenship."

"Lovely." Miranda sank into her chair. Her uncle
pilfered some paintings from a German museum, then
a half German shows up and wants, no, demands, to
buy the farm from her. And he'd even offered to pack
up Henry's things and have them sent to her. She grimaced. Robert Deverill had to know about the paintings. It was simply too much of a coincidence otherwise. The only question left was whether he was after
them for himself or for the German authorities. If he
wanted to resell them on the black market for his own
benefit, then he wouldn't want publicity any more than
she did. But if he were working for the government,
then he'd want credit for his discovery. Credit meant
publicity, lots of publicity.

"You okay?" Jenny asked. "You look kind of...tired."

"I'm fine. It's just that my mother came to tell me that
my uncle died," Miranda replied, giving her part of the
truth. "I'm going to have to go upstate for the funeral
and to settle his estate. Would you go down to the office and tell them not to accept specialized orders for me
until further notice, please?"

"Sure, and I'm sorry about your uncle." Jenny gave
her a sympathetic smile.

Miranda sat staring at the oak door Jenny had closed behind her, trying to plan a course of action, but found it impossible. Her mind was a curious jumble of sadness, excitement and dread. Mixed up in the middle of all those emotions was a man named Robert Deverill.

There was no doubt about it. She found him attractive. No, compelling, she amended. That worried her, because she knew almost nothing about him, and what little she did know told her he could well be a serious threat to her mother's future. So why didn't that knowledge extinguish the attraction?

What was it she wanted in a man? She'd never asked herself the question before, because it had never been relevant. Before she'd been married to Jim. She'd met him her first weekend at college. They'd simply drifted into a relationship, she'd found herself engaged, then married. It had just happened.

That had been her first mistake, she thought with the wisdom of hindsight. Allowing things to just happen. But it wasn't a mistake she would make again. She was no longer a naive seventeen. Before she got emotionally involved again, she would have a clear idea of exactly what it was she wanted in a man. She picked up a pencil and a pad of paper. What she needed was a list of qualities she considered essential. With a list she could weed out the unsuitable candidates before she invested a great deal of time and emotion.

So what did she want in a man? She gazed blankly at the wall, and an image of Robert's dark features superimposed itself. She wanted an attractive man, she decided. He didn't have to be classically handsome, just attractive to her.

What else? She tapped the pencil's eraser against her teeth. He needed to be physically in shape and financially self-sufficient. Never again was she going to allow some man to use her skill and talent to set himself up in business.

And he had to be sophisticated. One who wasn't bowled over by teenagers, she jotted down, remembering Brandy's youthful charms.

She also wanted a man whose profession was compatible with hers. That way they'd have lots in common. She felt a momentary pang as she recalled that Robert was a professional athlete, but firmly squelched it. Common interests were essential to any long-term relationship.

And her perfect man had to want at least one child. Jim had always claimed that the time wasn't quite right to start a family. Almost as if he'd known... She cut the thought off, refusing to dwell on the past. The future was what mattered.

Her ideal man had to be a generous, innovative lover, she wrote boldly. She was tired of mechanical lovemaking that left her feeling empty. A momentary doubt shook her when she remembered the one time, years ago, when she'd tried to tell Jim how dissatisfied she felt. He had brushed her remarks aside, telling her she simply wasn't a very sensual woman. That if he felt satisfied, then the problem had to be in her.

Maybe it had been, but she intended to explore the situation a little before she accepted Jim's negative assessment.

And he had to be kind. She wanted a relationship with a man who was nice, even when there was nothing in it for him. Patient, too. Impatient people were the pits to live with. And he had to be smart. Smart enough not to resent her own intelligence, as Jim often had. And he had to be an honorable man. She underlined the old-fashioned word. She refused to deal with a liar and a cheat again.

Miranda leaned back in her chair and studied the list for a moment, then grimaced. The man she'd just described sounded like a cross between Saint Thomas Aquinas and Patrick Swayze. She chuckled wryly. She should be so lucky.

"WELL?"

Robert jumped; the tall, blond man seemed to materialize beside him on the crowded sidewalk outside Felker and Felker.

"Axel, I swear I'm going to nominate you for the Invisible Man award," he grumbled.

"Stow the compliments and get to the point." Axel fell into step beside him. "Has she agreed to sell the farm to you?"

"No."

"Dammit! Why not?"

"She says she's going to live there."

"Live there!" Axel repeated incredulously. "Why would a longtime New Yorker suddenly want to live upstate?" He skirted a large woman walking an even larger dog. "What does this Miranda Sheffield look like?"

"She's got a figure straight out of a sexual fantasy, dark brown eyes full of intelligence and mystery, and silky, blond curls. A perfect playmate, as long as a man keeps his head. In fact, she reminds me a little of Inga." Robert heard his tone harden. "Not in looks, but in the innocence in her eyes that you'd swear was real."

"Do you think she knows about the stolen art?"

Robert shrugged. "Who knows? Nor do I know how we can find out what she knows. For that matter, what do we know?

"Really know," he added when Axel opened his mouth.

"Well..." Axel's deep voice trailed away into silence.

"Exactly. All we're sure of is that four years ago you recovered some jewelry stolen after the Second World War from a Stuttgart museum. When you questioned the woman who was trying to sell it, her defense was that you shouldn't confiscate her loot, because her dead husband's ex-sergeant took a whole lot more. You must admit, it hardly qualifies as a solid lead."

"I've tracked down missing art on a lot less," Axel insisted.

"And drawn a blank on a lot more," Robert countered. "You know damn well that even knowing Henry Sheffield was the sergeant she was referring to doesn't prove anything. Especially considering the fact that we haven't been able to tie him to any art—stolen or otherwise."

"True, but if it hadn't been for me tracking Sheffield back to his farm, you'd have never gone up there with me, and you'd have never found that ski lodge for sale. You owe me, Cousin."

"I know I'm in trouble when you start bringing our relationship into it. You know it's ironic, *Cousin,* but originally my trying to buy Henry's farm was simply an excuse to keep an eye on him. Now I really need that land."

"Which brings us full circle back to Ms. Sheffield. If only we knew whether she won't sell because she wants the farm or because she wants the art."

"While you're wishing, why don't you wish to know what the art actually is? It'd be nice to know what it is we're supposed to be looking for. Always provided, of course, that there really is any art and that woman simply wasn't trying to distract you."

"Ms. Sheffield's hurry to get up to the farm makes me believe that there really is something there." Axel clenched his fist. "If only you'd been there when Henry had his heart attack, instead of watching that damned tennis tournament in Nice, we could have searched the place before the lawyer stuck in that bucolic caretaker."

"Next time I'll remember not to accept any invitations," Robert said dryly. "At least you were able to get away from your business to check the situation out yourself. After all, you're the one who gets his kicks out of finding pilfered art. I'm just along for the ride."

"Well, unfortunately, this time you're driving, Cousin, because I absolutely have to get back to the Middle East. We're negotiating a very delicate contract with the Saudi government, and they expect to deal with the CEO himself. I won't be able to stay here more than another day or two, at the most.

"If there were just some way we could get into the farmhouse to search before Ms. Sheffield arrives, without making either the lawyer or the caretaker suspicious. The last thing we need is for the locals to think that there's something valuable hidden in Henry's house. We'd have every two-bit thief in a hundred-mile radius searching for the spoils."

Robert stopped in front of their parked rental car and considered the problem. "Why don't we have a woman call Henry's lawyer, identify herself as Miranda Sheffield, and tell him she'll be arriving in the morning and to have the caretaker gone by then?"

Axel weighed the idea. "It might work. It's certainly worth a try. I've got a friend who can make the call for us. With luck we should have several hours to search before she arrives."

"If we'd had any luck so far, we wouldn't be in this predicament," Robert said sourly.

2

MIRANDA CAREFULLY PULLED her compact car to the side of the deserted road and stared at the narrow track to her right. The minister who'd officiated at Henry's funeral had said her uncle's farm was half a mile down the third road on the right after she crossed the highway.

Which begged the question: was this deeply rutted, heavily iced path a road? There was no identifying signpost, but since it only led to her uncle's farm, the county might not have felt obligated to mark it.

Miranda looked around and shivered at the bleak, barren landscape visible in the afternoon's waning light. Upstate New York in November bore no relationship whatsoever to the luxuriant, verdant green of her summer childhood memories. This environment was hostile to man, almost aggressively so.

A sudden gust of wind swirled gently falling snowflakes against her windshield, prodding her into action. She decided to risk following the path for at least half a mile. Flipping on the windshield wipers, she very gently stepped on the gas and turned, having no desire to send the light car into a skid and wind up stuck in a ditch.

Five minutes later her decision was rewarded; she rounded a curve to discover a small cluster of buildings set back from the road. Miranda parked the car in front of the house and stared at it, vaguely perplexed. It was her uncle's farm and yet it wasn't. Somehow it seemed smaller than she remembered. Smaller and much shabbier. But she reminded herself she hadn't been here for almost fifteen years. Not since the summer she'd graduated from high school and her parents had finally agreed on a divorce.

She climbed out of the car. The inside of the house was probably exactly as she remembered it, she encouraged herself. She was wrong. Although, in truth, it was hard to tell exactly what it did look like in the light that filtered in through the dusty windows.

Miranda sighed, putting a white puff of breath into the house's frigid air. She was filled with an overwhelming sense of sadness. For a second she wished she hadn't come, that she had left her remembrances of those summer visits shining brightly in her memory.

"No," she muttered. Reality was always better than dreams, no matter how pleasant the dreams might have been. All the place needed was a thorough cleaning and it would be as good as new. But not this afternoon. This afternoon she didn't feel capable of coping with anything. The long drive from New York City in an unfamiliar car over icy roads, followed by the emotional turmoil of her uncle's funeral, had completely drained her energy. All she felt capable of doing at the moment was taking a bath and falling into bed.

She flipped on the light switch beside the front door. Nothing happened. Walking to the table lamp beside a well-worn armchair, she turned it on. Again nothing happened.

Miranda checked to make sure there was a bulb in the lamp. She tried tightening it, but it made no difference. The room remained discouragingly dim. Fearing it was hopeless, but determined to try, Miranda went through each of the farmhouse's four rooms, flipping switches.

It was patently obvious that there was no electricity. Had the power company turned it off when her uncle died? She shivered as a puff of icy air slithered down her neck. Would the lack of electricity also account for the lack of heat? she wondered. Did furnaces depend on electricity to work?

Miranda ran her fingers through her short curls in frustration. Maybe it wasn't the power company's fault, she decided, remembering the caretaker. He must have been using electricity. Maybe he'd switched it off when he left. Maybe getting the power turned on was simply a matter of flipping another switch. She looked around the small kitchen, wondering where to find the circuit-breaker box. Or, more likely, considering the age of the house, the fuse box.

Unable to find it on the main floor, she opened the basement door and found herself staring down into a pit of stygian blackness from which rose eddies of damp, mildew-tainted air. And, much more ominously, sounds of movement.

The hair on Miranda's arms lifted as she caught a muffled curse. "Who's there?" she demanded, then could have cried a second later at the stupidity of the question. If she had simply pretended not to have noticed anything amiss, she could have closed the basement door and escaped.

At the sound of heavy footsteps on the stairs she looked wildly around the kitchen for something to use to defend herself, knowing there was no way she could outrun anyone in her high-heeled boots.

"Is that you, Miranda?" The blessedly familiar tones of Robert Deverill's voice poured soothingly over her fear-stretched nerves. For a moment, relief that she wasn't in any physical danger made her light-headed, but when Robert appeared in the doorway, a sudden gust of anger made her tremble.

How dare he frighten her out of her wits like that? If she'd had a weak heart, she'd be lying on the floor, dead.

"What the hell are you doing, skulking around in my basement?" she yelled at him. "You—" Miranda stopped when a tall, blond man emerged from behind Robert.

Miranda eyed the stranger uncertainly, measuring his erect bearing and arrogant expression. He might be wearing jeans and a ski jacket, but he had power and authority stamped all over him.

"Who's your partner in crime?" she demanded, covering her fear with aggression.

"My cousin, Axel von Maltzan."

Miranda felt her heart sink; she recognized the name. She'd read an article in *The Wall Street Journal* last year about how he'd recovered some antique jewelry stolen during the partitioning of Berlin. Cousin or not, if Axel von Maltzan was involved, the German government had to know about the paintings. But they hadn't found them yet. She breathed an inward sigh of relief when she realized that the only things the two men were carrying were flashlights. "Tell me, did you meet him down there or did you bring him along?" she snapped.

"Along," Robert said, mentally scrambling for a plausible lie to account for being in her basement. That must have been the shortest funeral in history. She shouldn't have been back for over an hour.

"Well?"

"Actually, Miranda," Robert said when Axel remained silent, "I didn't think you'd mind, since you weren't here."

"You thought wrong."

"I wanted to show Axel an authentic American basement," he improvised. "You see, he's an interior decorator."

"An interior decorator!" Miranda stared at Axel. He hadn't moved a muscle, but she'd have bet her last dollar that he was trying to restrain a smirk.

"Yes. I want him to design a bar in my basement with an Early American flavor, and it doesn't get much earlier than Henry's house," Robert continued doggedly.

Fascinated, Miranda studied the pair. If her stepfather's career wasn't hanging in the balance, the whole situation would be hilarious. Inspecting basements for ideas for bars? What kind of government agents were they? She would have thought they'd have figured out a cover story beforehand. Unfortunately, despite the transparency of their lie, she didn't dare risk a confrontation. As long as they thought she didn't know what they were up to, she had time. Time to find the paintings first.

"How did you get here?" she demanded, suddenly remembering that there hadn't been another car parked in front of the house.

"I parked behind the barn," Robert answered.

Where his car wouldn't be seen, Miranda concluded. What on earth had she gotten herself into? At least there weren't any bloody corpses involved. So far.

"But since we have disturbed you, we can only offer our apologies and leave," Robert said apologetically, practically dragging his companion out the door.

"Good afternoon, Frau Sheffield." Axel gave her a gleaming smile that did nothing to warm the arctic coldness of his gray eyes. She had no trouble believing the article's claim that Axel von Maltzan could be absolutely ruthless in the pursuit of a goal.

And so could she. She tried to rally her flagging spirits, shivering as she glanced around the room. "The health department would have a spasm if they could see this place," she muttered in disgust. Tomorrow morning she would disinfect everything, but first she had to get through the night. Perhaps . . . She remembered the sign she'd passed about half a mile before the turnoff. It had been for a ski lodge. The sign had been in excellent condition, as had the freshly plowed road beside it. Maybe she could get a room there until Monday, when the power company would be open, and she could find out how the electricity in the house operated, or, more accurately, didn't.

She decided to wait a few minutes to be sure Robert and his cohort had really gone. Once she felt it was safe, she left the house, shivering again when the icy, snow-filled wind lying in wait outside pounced upon her defenseless body. Hurrying, she slipped on a patch of ice on the steps and barely saved herself from a fall by grabbing hold of the rickety railing. To her relief, it held.

Moving more cautiously, she made her way toward her bright red car, which was now covered with a light dusting of snow. Miranda hurriedly brushed off the windshield and slipped inside, turning up the heater. She rubbed her numb fingers in the blast of hot air and added warm clothing to her list of items to be acquired without delay. Her leather boots and cropped leather jacket might be the latest fashion statement, but left a lot to be desired in the warmth department.

Miranda turned the car in the narrow space in front of the house and made her way toward the main road. The gusting wind was beginning to cause the snow to drift, making the car slip and slide on the now-hidden patches of ice.

Once she reached the highway, the going was much easier, and she arrived at the ski lodge without further mishap. She pulled into the almost full parking lot, cut the engine and looked around with interest.

The main building had been constructed at the top of a gentle rise at the north end of the parking lot. Behind it, the Adirondack Mountains loomed protectively.

Very nice, Miranda thought as she studied the huge, three-storied colonial structure approvingly. It was immense and, in stark contrast to her uncle's farmhouse, in perfect repair. The white paint gleamed in the deepening twilight, and the dark green shutters on the oversize windows added a pleasing visual contrast. The small, squat evergreens that dotted the front lawn had been generously hung with fairy lights that twinkled welcomingly.

Miranda smiled happily at the sight. The lights reminded her of childhood Christmases, when relationships had been clearly defined and easy to understand. Her lips twisted bitterly. Now she knew better. Nothing was ever simple, and the one relationship she'd thought secure had shattered at the first smile from Brandy. Briefly closing her eyes, she forced the painful memory to the back of her mind. While she was up here she was going to concentrate on finding the paintings. That, at least, was a problem she could solve. In fact, she felt a sudden surge of revitalizing adrenaline—she'd enjoy defeating Robert Deverill.

Locking her car doors, she carefully crossed the sanded parking lot and stepped into the brightly lit, spacious lobby. Her eyes were drawn to the roaring fire burning in the immense fieldstone fireplace to her right. At least fifteen people in colorful ski sweaters were gathered around it, munching cheese and crackers from the tray on the coffee table.

Miranda swallowed hungrily. The roads had been so bad that she hadn't stopped for lunch, determined to be on time for the funeral. Just as soon as she registered, she was going to eat, she promised her grumbling stomach and headed toward the reception desk.

"Yes? May I help you?" A comfortably plump, middle-aged woman smiled welcomingly.

"I sure hope so. Mrs. Read," Miranda said, reading the name tag the woman was wearing, "I need a room for a few days."

"Oh, dear." Mrs. Read's smile faded. "That's going to present a problem."

Miranda sighed. "I was afraid of that when I saw how full the parking lot was."

"We certainly are busy," Mrs. Read declared with obvious pride. "We're booked solid through the end of the season, although one of our guests did call a few hours ago to say he wouldn't be able to use his reservation until tomorrow afternoon. I could let you have his room for tonight."

"Sounds great," Miranda said, relieved that she wasn't going to have to face those icy roads until tomorrow. "I really appreciate it."

Mrs. Read handed her a reservation card. "Our other guest will appreciate it, too. This way he won't have to pay for a room he didn't use."

She handed Miranda a key. "You're in Room 315. Take the elevator to the third floor and turn to your right."

Smiling at the helpful woman, Miranda pocketed the key and headed for the parking lot to get her suitcase.

Thirty minutes later, after a quick shower, she was back downstairs. At barely five o'clock, the dining room was virtually empty, and Miranda, in response to a sign telling her to please be seated, chose a table for two beside one of the huge, multipaned windows.

A friendly young waitress handed her a menu, asked if she wanted a drink and, upon Miranda's refusal, left her to consider her choice for dinner, a process that unfortunately didn't require much effort. The menu lacked both variety and interest, leaning heavily toward hearty entrées full of cholesterol and starch.

Perhaps with good reason. Miranda glanced around with a professional eye, noting that the few diners there looked to be in their mid-twenties. Maybe hearty meals were what skiers wanted after a long, tiring day on the slopes.

Choosing what appeared to be the leanest cut of meat on the limited menu, she ordered roast beef, and was told by the waitress to help herself from the salad bar. She found it tucked in an alcove. It consisted of an extensive collection of fresh fruits and vegetables, but they weren't well presented. They lacked the visual additions that denoted a first-class establishment. This place was a rather curious mixture, Miranda thought. No expense seemed to have been spared in what was served, but no thought given to how it was presented.

Her meal, when it came, was tasty. The baked potato was steaming hot and the meat juicy, tender and the portion large. But again there was no garnish on the plate of any sort. Not even a sprig of parsley.

When Miranda had finished, she picked up the dessert menu. The meager list was headed by rice pudding and ended three entries later with lemon meringue pie.

"Why the frown? You certainly can't be on a diet with a figure like yours."

Miranda looked up into the appreciative gaze of Robert Deverill's hazel eyes. She mentally added to her list. A voice just like his. Like dusk on a soft, summer evening. Warm and dark and full of surprises.

"What are you doing here?" she asked, wondering for one wild moment if they'd waited on the road and followed her. He'd said he lived in the area, but it was stretching coincidence for him to be here at the lodge at precisely the same time she was. "And where's your accomplice?"

"My cousin had to leave for the airport the minute we got back." He sat down across from her and gestured toward the waitress.

"Sally, I'd like a cup of coffee, and Miranda would like . . ." He looked at her.

"A piece of lemon meringue pie," she filled in.

With a smile, Sally hurried away, and Miranda turned back to Robert. "How did you know I was here?" she asked, wondering if she could believe him about Axel's whereabouts.

"Maud. Mrs. Read at the reception desk," he elaborated at her blank look. "She mentioned that we'd had an unexpected guest, and I checked your registration card."

"Well, that explains how you happen to be here in the dining room, but not how you happened to be here in the inn," she persisted.

"I live here. I own the lodge. That's why I need your farm."

"Of course." Miranda nodded, not believing a word he said.

"I really—" He paused as Sally slid Miranda's piece of pie in front of her, then served his coffee.

"What's the matter?" He watched as Miranda tentatively poked the soggy piecrust.

"When was the last time you ate anything from your dessert menu?" she asked.

"Never," he said smugly. "I don't eat sweets."

"Probably a wise choice under the circumstances. This thing masquerading as a piece of pie belongs in a greasy spoon, not a first-class resort."

"You haven't even tasted it," Robert protested.

"I don't need to. The crust is soggy, the meringue is weeping, and I'll lay you odds the filling came out of a box." She put her fork upon the plate and pushed it aside.

"Fortunately, not all my guests are as picky as you."

"That's because you have a captive audience."

"You're being overly critical. Just because you cook—"

"I don't cook, I bake," she corrected him. "And I'm very good at what I do. I also happen to have a degree from Cornell's School of Hotel Management."

"You do?" He looked surprised. "Then why aren't you in charge of the kitchens of a big hotel somewhere?"

"Because I can think of nothing more boring than having to spend my time balancing books and fighting with suppliers." *As Jim loves to do.* The thought crossed her mind, followed by the appalling realization that if she did buy out Jim's half of the business, those jobs would fall to her. Even if she hired someone to do them, she'd still have to cut back on her baking time in order to supervise, or she could find herself robbed blind.

"Tell me why it follows that owning this place also necessitates owning my farm?" she asked, trying to find out all she could while she had the chance.

"Your farm is the only property that borders my lodge that is not part of the Adirondack State Park."

Miranda frowned. "Has anyone ever told you that you have a positive genius for non sequiturs?"

"I want to expand."

"I see," she said slowly, not knowing whether to believe him or not. His so-called expansion could be just an excuse to get the farm without anyone asking any awkward questions. Or he could have two separate agendas.

"Your farm is perfect," he continued.

"I don't see how," she said suspiciously. "Most of it's flat, and the few hills there are would be pretty tame skiing, even for a rank beginner."

"Actually it would be perfect for some cross-country ski trails, but what I really want it for is the summer."

He leaned forward, and Miranda caught a very faint whiff of his cologne. The musky fragrance teased her mind, distracting her from what he was saying. She looked at his mouth in an attempt to concentrate and, instead, was distracted by the shape of his lips, wondering how they would feel against hers....

"...excellent price," he continued, and Miranda pulled her eyes away. "Business has been so good that I've decided to go with my original plans and remain open all year round. To do that I need more land. More level land," he amended. "And that's where your farm comes in. I could put in family cabins, a riding stable, swimming pools, tennis courts and hiking trails. All the things that people expect from a summer resort."

"Original plans?" Miranda latched onto the words.

"Uh-huh. When I inspected this place before I bought it, I looked into the possibility of eventually expanding it to a year-round facility," he told her.

"You should have found out then that you were virtually surrounded by public land."

"I did. I went to talk to Henry, and we had a gentleman's agreement. He said he was planning on retiring to Florida in a few years. And that he'd give me first right of refusal on his farm, if I would supply him with dinner from the dining room here and keep his driveway plowed in the winter."

Miranda frowned again, wondering how much was fabrication. The only one who could tell her for certain was Henry, and he was dead.

"Your farm—"

"Do you know why my electricity is turned off?" she inquired, determinedly changing the subject.

"More than likely there's a part loose, or else it's empty," he lied. He and Axel had disabled the generator in the hope that without electricity, she'd decide to stay at the motel in town, which would have given them all night to search. What they hadn't counted on was the unexpected vacancy here at the inn—or the urgent message, demanding that Axel return to the Middle East immediately.

"Empty?" she repeated blankly.

"Yes, you know, empty. The generator. It runs on gas."

"No, I didn't know. I thought I got my electricity from the electric company like every other normal consumer."

"A generator's perfectly reliable if you keep it serviced."

"Do you know how to service one?" Miranda asked, feeling that he owed her something for scaring her out of her wits earlier.

Robert did his best to squelch his feeling of satisfaction. With any luck at all, he should be able to finish looking around the basement in the guise of checking the generator. But it wouldn't do to seem too eager, or she might suspect his motives.

"Give me one good reason why I should help you," he finally said, studying the velvety softness of her large brown eyes. She really was a beautiful woman. In fact, for some reason she reminded him of the mistress his grandfather had had the summer he himself had been fifteen. He smiled cynically, remembering his adolescent ravings about the woman's beauty and his naive query as to whether his grandfather was going to marry her. The older man had laughed and said that marriage had to do with respect and family and money, not with beauty or sex or love.

"You're a kindhearted soul who doesn't want to see me stumbling around in the dark?" Miranda wondered at his smile. She didn't like it. It wasn't a warm smile that invited you to share the joke. There was something chilling about it, as if he knew something you didn't.

Robert shook off the past with an effort. "But if it's dark I won't see you, will I?"

"You'll hear me when I scream," she muttered. "Tell you what, I'll trade you."

"Now this is getting interesting." The sudden gleam in his eyes brought her an answering surge of warmth.

"My expert knowledge of baking," she said repressively.

He grimaced. "I already have a cook. She's even temperamental."

"Considering how she bakes, you're the one who should be temperamental. I'd be willing to demonstrate a few simple dessert recipes in exchange for getting my generator started tomorrow."

"All right, I'll accept your trade," he finally said, trying to sound casual. "I'll start your generator tomorrow, and you can show my cook a couple of recipes. But don't you dare upset her," he warned. "Good cooks willing to work in the Adirondacks are hard to find."

Miranda glanced at the soggy pie. "Yes, I can see that."

3

"I HOPE YOU ENJOYED your stay with us, Ms. Sheffield?" Maud smiled warmly at Miranda.

"The room was very comfortable." *Even if the same can't be said about the owner,* Miranda thought.

Maud chuckled. "Skiers like to consider themselves rugged sportsmen, but when it comes to creature comforts, they demand the best." She handed Miranda the copy of her credit card receipt.

Miranda smiled. "Don't we all. Could you tell me where to buy supplies?"

"If you mean skiing supplies, our shop to the left of the entrance carries everything you could ever need."

"No, I need cleaning supplies and food, stuff like that."

Maud was clearly puzzled. "What are you planning to do?"

"Commit an act of idiocy." Robert's deep voice startled Miranda. Slowly, giving herself time to regain her normal poise, she turned. The sight of him did nothing to help. His dark brown hair was slightly disheveled, and his cheeks had a reddish tinge, as if he'd just come in from outside. Her fingers itched to touch his face to see if it really was as chilled as it looked. She curled her fingers into a fist.

"Good morning, Robert. This is Ms. Sheffield."

"Also known as Old Henry's niece. And she's every bit as stubborn as he was," Robert confided in an audible aside.

"I am not!" Miranda objected, mentally adding to her list. Reasonable. She wanted a man who was open and aboveboard and reasonable. One who didn't skulk in basements and tell improbable lies that a six-year-old could see through.

Maud glanced from Miranda to Robert in confusion. "Did I miss something?" she finally asked.

"Miranda is the one missing something—common sense."

Miranda shoved her credit receipt into her jacket pocket; the familiar sense of frustration filled her. There was just enough truth in his charge to hurt. She hadn't even realized that her own husband was sneaking around behind her back until he'd asked for a divorce. She tightened her lips. She not only lacked common sense, she must have been brain dead to have missed all the signs.

"I've got lots of common sense," she finally said. "It's what protects me from letting you take advantage of me."

"Oh, no, Ms. Sheffield." Maud leaned across the counter, clearly eager to convince Miranda. "Robert would never take advantage of anyone. Why, he's as honest as the day is long."

"If I remember correctly, the shortest day of the year is fast approaching," Miranda said tartly. "Now, then—" she ignored both Maud's outraged gasp and Robert's unexpected chuckle "—if you could just tell me where to go . . ."

"Tempting," Robert murmured. "Very tempting."

Miranda gave him the repressive look she'd found useful in the training of cocksure, new pastry chefs. The only impression it seemed to have on him was to deepen the dimple in his left cheek. Valiantly ignoring it, she continued. "To buy supplies."

"No need for that." Maud seemed glad to have a nonpersonal subject to discuss. "We've got tons of cleaning supplies here. Since you're a neighbor, we can fix you up with what you need, can't we, Robert?"

"Of course." He gave the only response possible without making Maud suspicious. He'd hoped to be able to search the farmhouse while Miranda was in town, buying supplies. Ah, well, he consoled himself, he'd be able to take a quick look around this afternoon when he fixed her generator. If he was lucky, he'd find something incriminating and, once he did that, he could get a search warrant issued.

"Thank you," Miranda said, amused at the position Maud's spontaneous generosity had put him in. The poor man was being forced to give aid and comfort to the enemy. She found it interesting that Maud had felt free to make the offer. Under normal circumstances, Robert must be a very generous man. She stifled a sigh. Unfortunately, there was nothing even vaguely normal about this situation.

"And that'll save you from going out on the roads until the county has had a chance to clear them," Maud continued. "We had almost three inches of new snow last night. You'll want to take it easy until you're used to driving in winter conditions."

"If you'll come with me." Robert started down the hallway to his left.

Giving the curious Maud a quick smile, Miranda followed him, stopping in front of a white-paneled door. She tensed as he reached around her to push it open. His wool-clad arm brushed against her cheek; beneath the sweater's exquisite softness she could feel hard muscles.

Eager to put some distance between them, without being obvious about it, she hastily walked through the open door. She looked around with unfeigned delight. A great deal of planning had obviously gone into creating this spacious, highly efficient workplace. As well as a great deal of money. Miranda noted the abundance of high-quality equipment.

A gaunt woman somewhere between fifty and sixty glanced up from the huge stockpot she was stirring. She studied Miranda before turning to Robert and demanding, "What do you want? I'm busy with lunch preparations."

To Miranda's surprise, Robert ignored the woman's dismissive manner. "We won't bother you, Mrs. Kolcheck."

Aha! Miranda thought. *The temperamental cook.* She eyed the woman curiously. Was it really that hard to find cooks willing to work up here in the winter, or was there another reason Robert put up with her curtness? Could Mrs. Kolcheck know something Robert didn't want to become common knowledge?

On the surface it didn't seem probable but then, she would never have believed her uncle had been an art thief. It couldn't be anything from Robert's past, or the scandal sheets would have long since ferreted it out. Maybe Mrs. Kolcheck knew something about him of more recent vintage? Something about her uncle? Even something about the paintings? It didn't seem too likely. On the other hand, it wouldn't hurt to sound the woman out when she got a chance, Miranda decided.

Robert introduced them. "This is Miss Sheffield, Mrs. Kolcheck. She's going to come by tomorrow and demonstrate a few dessert recipes."

"She's what?" Mrs. Kolcheck stopped stirring and looked up, her glance pinning Robert to the floor. She put her hands upon her nonexistent hips and glared at him. "And what, pray tell, is wrong with the way I cook?"

"Absolutely nothing," Robert said soothingly. "You're—"

"Mr. Deverill—" a young man stuck his head through the kitchen door "—could you come into the ski shop a minute? Some lady wants to charge twelve hundred dollars' worth of equipment, and her credit card won't accept it."

Robert glanced at Miranda. She shrugged and said, "Go ahead. I'm in no hurry."

Mrs. Kolcheck waited until the door had swung shut behind Robert, then snapped, "I don't know what you think you could tell me about cooking."

"Nothing," Miranda said. "I don't cook. I bake. Wedding cakes are my specialty."

"Bah!" Mrs. Kolcheck snorted. "All those fancy furbelows. I don't hold with frills." She glared at Miranda. "Good, plain cooking, that's all a body needs."

"It may be all a body needs or even all they deserve, but is it all they want?" Miranda asked mildly.

"I'm not gonna—"

"Please don't refuse." Miranda gave Mrs. Kolcheck her best "me against the world" smile. A smile that seemed to come naturally these days. "I'm desperate to get my electricity turned on, and if you refuse to let me demonstrate some recipes, I won't."

"Huh?" Mrs. Kolcheck eyed her blankly. "What's electricity got to do with anything?"

"I'm going to be living on my Uncle Henry's farm."

"Henry Sheffield was a cantankerous old goat, always telling me that I didn't put enough salt in my cooking, but that still doesn't tell me nothing about any electricity."

"I need Robert to fix the farm's generator, so I can have lights, and he only agreed to do it if I did something for him. The only thing I could think of to do was to demonstrate some recipes."

"Hmph! The wonder is that he couldn't think of something else for you to do. Pretty little thing like you." Mrs. Kolcheck eyed her speculatively.

"Thank you."

"No call to thank me. I wasn't the one who gave you them looks. The good Lord did. He—" Robert came back.

"Miss Sheffield here explained everything, and I guess it's all right." Mrs. Kolcheck didn't sound any too certain. "You come by tomorrow after lunch," she told Miranda. "I got time then to listen."

"Thank you, and we'll want Mr. Deverill to come, too, so that he can appreciate what's involved." Miranda eyed him narrowly. There was no way she was going to spend the afternoon here and leave her house unprotected.

Dammit, Robert thought in frustration. Of all the times for Axel to be embroiled in a business crisis. Searching for that art was a two-man job. He could hardly keep Miranda out of the way and search for it at the same time. On the other hand, he didn't want to refuse and make her any more suspicious than she already was. If she felt pushed, she might call in a friend to help her look. A woman as gorgeous as she was would be bound to have some gullible male on a string somewhere to do her bidding.

"I'll look forward to it," he muttered. "Come on. Let's get your stuff."

Miranda suppressed a smile at her victory and followed him into a large supply room. "What time are you coming to fix my generator?" she asked, wanting an idea of when to expect him so that he didn't catch her searching. He might have his suspicions about her motives for being here, but he couldn't be certain. That meant she had the advantage.

All she had to do was to be careful not to give him cause to think that she was a threat to his plans. Which probably wouldn't be that hard, she thought sadly. No one seemed to find her much of a challenge. Not Robert and Axel with their harebrained excuses, nor her ex-husband, and certainly not his new wife.

"Cheer up," Robert said, seeing her wistful expression. "I'll be over to reconnect your lights after the lunch rush is over."

"Reconnect?" Miranda jumped on the word. Had he and his henchman sabotaged her power?

"Reconnect, fix, repair." He tried to retrieve his slip. He was going to have to be careful. It was becoming increasingly clear that there was a whole lot more to Miranda Sheffield than her sexy exterior. She had a razor-sharp mind that missed very little. Beauty and brains were a lethal combination. Fortunately, he was forewarned.

Maud stuck her head around the supply room door. "There's a long-distance call for you. It's Axel. He says it's important," she added when Robert hesitated.

"I'll be right there." He started toward the door, then turned back to Miranda. "Fill one of those empty boxes on the bottom shelf with whatever food you want. I'll send Dave to carry it out to your car for you."

Miranda stared after him with a sinking feeling. Axel might not be physically present, but it would appear he was still very much involved in the search for the missing art. She wondered uneasily what he had to report.

Quickly she began to fill the box Robert had given her. She needed to get back to the farmhouse and find those paintings before the conspirators.

BY TWO THAT AFTERNOON Miranda was beginning to realize that things weren't going to be quite that easy.

She felt as if she'd been cleaning for years, not hours. She'd pushed and shoved, scrubbed, dusted or swept every surface in the small farmhouse. Strangely enough, she'd found a great deal of satisfaction in the exhausting work. She could see the results of her efforts, and that in turn momentarily soothed the feeling of helplessness that seemed to have dogged her ever since her husband had so unexpectedly demanded a divorce to—as he had put it—"marry my one true love."

Miranda snorted inelegantly. Until that moment, she'd never realized that Jim had harbored an almost maudlin romantic streak. She stared blindly out the gleaming windows. In fact, in the weeks that had followed his declaration, she'd discovered a whole lot of things she hadn't known about Jim and hadn't much liked. Why had it taken her so long to really look at the man she'd married?

Through the living-room window she caught a flash of movement in the trees. A black pickup was coming along the narrow road from the lodge. Robert?

She went into the kitchen and set the old-fashioned Graniteware coffeepot she'd filled earlier upon the stove, then hurried back into the living room. If it was Robert, he'd probably appreciate a hot drink. If it wasn't . . . Her eyes strayed to the hunting rifle lying on the coffee table. She'd found it when she'd cleaned under her uncle's bed and, while she had no more than a sketchy idea of how to use it, she'd hoped that the sight of it would be enough to discourage a would-be burglar.

Her trepidation turned to anticipation when she saw it was Robert. The worn denim of his jeans lovingly

molded the backs of his muscular thighs and flat hips
as he exited the truck.

Miranda ran the tip of her tongue over her suddenly
dry lips as he turned; she found her gaze focusing on his
flat abdomen. Her eyes dropped to linger on the slight
swell at the juncture of his thighs.

She started to pull her imagination up short, then
stopped. She was a free agent. If she wanted to look,
she'd look, and if she wanted to kiss him, she'd kiss him.
And if she wanted to make love with him . . .

The sound of his footsteps echoing on her wooden
porch interrupted her thoughts, and she opened the
door, wincing as an arctic blast froze the air in her
lungs.

"Hurry up," she gasped, grabbing the box he clasped
in his arms, then almost dropping it. It weighed a ton.
Miranda staggered to the coffee table and set it down.

"What on earth do you have in here?" she asked.

"I'm not sure. Mrs. Kolcheck sent it over. I think she
feels sorry for you. She said . . ." He paused as he saw
the gun on the table. He set down the large, gray metal
toolbox he had been carrying in his other hand and
picked up the hunting rifle, being careful to keep it
aimed toward the floor.

"What are you doing with this thing?" he demanded. "You could shoot yourself and bleed to death
before anyone was the wiser."

"Hardly," Miranda scoffed, much more interested in the contents of the box. She sat down on the floor and began to sift through it.

"I want to know what you are planning on doing with this thing," he persisted.

Miranda stopped rummaging and peered up at him. He seemed even bigger and much more masculine. She forced her eyes to focus on his face. The snowflakes dotting his hair were beginning to melt, adding a diamond glitter to his dark hair.

"Well?"

"I was hoping that the sight of it would frighten intruders away," she said dryly, "but I can see I was overly optimistic."

"I don't know about intruders, but the sight of this rifle would give any rational person the shakes."

Miranda gave him a saccharine smile. "Since I am the only rational person here and I'm not the least bit scared..."

"The thought of you playing cops and robbers with one of Henry's guns scares me enough for both of us," he said emphatically.

"Oh, for heaven's sake!" Miranda got to her feet. "I don't know why it is that men always seem to think that women are total idiots when it comes to guns. I've got more sense than to load the blasted thing, but since the very sight of it seems to bother you, I'll just—" She grabbed the gun around the barrel.

Robert's shout was drowned by the earsplitting roar of the discharging rifle.

Miranda let go of the gun as if scalded and jumped back in horror. Her eyes flew to Robert and she fearfully searched his body for gaping holes. To her infinite relief there were none.

"What happened?" she gasped, coughing; the acrid smell of gunpowder filled her nostrils.

"What happened!" Robert yelled at her. "The *unloaded* gun went off! Any idiot knows not to pick up a gun near the trigger."

"I didn't," she muttered, feeling like the idiot he'd called her. While she might not have ever actually held a gun, she had watched enough news broadcasts to know how dangerous guns could be.

"I stand corrected!" he retorted. "All the idiots except one know."

"But I never loaded it," she said, trying to defend herself, shivering as she remembered the cavalier way she'd handled the weapon earlier. She was extremely lucky she hadn't shot herself.

"It didn't occur to you to check and see if Henry had?" he asked scathingly. "At the rate you're going, all I'm going to have to do is wait for you to kill yourself and I can buy the farm from your next of kin."

Next of kin? Kill herself? The words echoed through Miranda's still-shocked mind. Nervously she studied his face. His jaws were clenched, and the corded muscles showed clearly under his deeply tanned skin. His lips were pressed together, and his eyes glittered greenly with the force of the emotion gripping him. Anger, she labeled it, relaxing slightly. Robert was furiously, blazingly angry, but he wasn't homicidal.

Besides, she admitted honestly, he had every right to be mad at her. She could have killed him. She definitely owed him an apology.

Taking a deep breath, she said, "I'm sorry if my actions upset you."

"Upset me!" he repeated incredulously. She hadn't upset him, he thought grimly. She'd frightened him out of his mind. For one terrifying moment he'd thought that bullet had struck her, and the fear he'd felt had momentarily frozen his thought processes. He wanted to make her understand just what a narrow escape she'd had. Failing that, he wanted to vent his feelings by taking her into his arms and kissing her senseless. Knowing that he was overreacting, Robert made a conscious effort to douse his anger.

"As you say, you aren't used to guns. And that being the case, I think I'll take this one home with me."

"No," she said succinctly.

"But . . ."

"Now that I know the thing has a hair trigger, I'll be more careful. But I need some protection out here, all by myself. Someone might try to break in. Someone besides you and your accomplice," she added dryly. "Now, shall we see about getting me some lights?"

Careful, be damned! he thought. He'd bet every penny he owned that Miranda Sheffield didn't have a careful bone in her body. Flinging guns around as if they were cap pistols and demanding to know who was in her basement, when a more fearful soul would have run for her life at the first sound.

No, Miranda Sheffield was not a cautious person. She rushed to experience life with an eagerness that seemed to border on the foolhardy. He clenched his fingers as he studied the soft, pink swell of her lower lip. Would she bring that same impulsiveness to bed? He didn't know, but wanted to find out. He'd have to be careful, though. Miranda Sheffield was not turning out to be at all what he had expected. In fact, other than giving him a few sidelong glances, she hadn't reacted to him at all. Why? Because she was emotionally involved with another man? Or because he simply didn't turn her on? He found both alternatives unacceptable.

"I really will be careful," Miranda offered placatingly, breaking the silence that had changed somehow, becoming charged with an emotion she couldn't quite put a name to. All she knew for certain was that it made her feel distinctly unsettled.

"Well," he finally said, "I'd better get started, or you really will be stumbling around in the dark."

It would take a lot more than a working generator, Miranda reflected, to get herself out of this darkness.

4

MIRANDA PAUSED when she heard a thump from the basement. She crept toward the heat register in the kitchen floor and leaned closer, straining to hear, but it was impossible to tell which of the various squeaks and bumps were coming from the ancient furnace and which were being made by Robert.

She could hear the sound of scraping; it was as if something were being dragged along the basement's stone floor. She closed her eyes, trying to remember the layout. Where was the generator? The west wall was covered with shelves of canning jars. Opposite them was the furnace.... Her eyes flew open. That was a wood-burning furnace. A wood-burning furnace that generated a great deal of heat. There couldn't possibly be a gas-powered anything in the basement, or it would have exploded long before now.

She pressed her lips together in self-disgust at her gullibility. Even if Robert hadn't known the generator wasn't in the basement, one quick look should have told him. It would hardly have taken him twenty minutes to figure it out. So what was he doing down there? Undoubtedly searching for her paintings.

Tiptoeing across the floor so as not to alert him to her movements, she eased open the basement door. The scuffling sounds coming from below would drown any noise she was making. With the finesse of a seasoned cat burglar, she crept down the steps.

Miranda paused in the shadows on the third step and peered down. Robert had set a battery-operated lantern upon a box, and its glow was a welcome addition to the small amount of sunlight filtering through the two tiny windows on the north and south walls.

She narrowed her eyes and watched him closely. His back was to her, and he was bent over a box, rifling its contents. Her eyes lingered on his broad shoulders, and she felt a strange twisting sensation in the region on her stomach, making her want to touch him. Then, Robert uttered a brief curse at something he found in the box and the unexpected sound broke the strange spell.

What on earth was the matter with her? She'd never ogled men's bodies. In fact, she had always felt an impatient pity for women who seemed obsessed by a man's physical presence. She certainly had never felt this strange compulsion to touch her ex-husband. Not that she'd found Jim physically repulsive, because she hadn't. It was simply that touching him, indeed, kissing him had always been a mildly pleasant activity and nothing more. Had Jim felt the same way about her? she wondered. Had he looked at Brandy and experienced the same compulsion to touch that she'd just felt toward Robert? Maybe she simply wasn't the kind of woman who inspired that kind of reaction in a man. It was a sobering thought, and the fear that she might be right goaded her to speak.

"Let me guess. It's a portable generator, which is why you're looking in boxes."

Robert jerked around. "Actually, I was searching for..." His voice tailed away; once again he was scrambling for a plausible explanation.

"Yes?" Miranda murmured, beginning to enjoy herself. Robert must not do much lying. He was too bad at it to have had much practice.

"Mice," he finally said. "I was searching for signs of rodent infestation."

"You weren't willing to settle for the mouse droppings on top of the boxes?" she asked dryly.

"Mice can be a real problem," he continued doggedly.

"Among other things. Tell me, have you found the generator yet?"

"Oh, it isn't down here."

"Then why are you down here? Again," she added.

"Because the lead from the generator is." He gestured toward a small, gray box on the wall. "I already fixed it, and once I clean the generator's motor and fill it with gas, you should have lights."

"Where exactly is this generator that you're going to fill up?" she asked in exasperation.

"In the barn, of course."

"Of course," she muttered. "I should have realized that the minute you headed for the basement."

"You know," he went on, "I think you've got dry rot."

"If it weren't for the fact that my mother told me never to make personal comments, I'd tell you what I think you've got," Miranda said virtuously.

"Not you. Your rafters." He gestured toward the exposed floor beams above his head. "It's a real problem in old houses like this."

"You can drop the scare tactics. I'm not going to sell."

"But this place could be dangerous. It—"

"Never!" she insisted melodramatically. "This is my birthright. Why, did you know that there's been a Sheffield here since before the Revolutionary War? This land is a sacred trust. A memorial to future generations!"

Robert snorted in audible disgust. "Might I point out to you that in order to have the next generation, you have to first get remarried, in which case your name wouldn't be Sheffield anymore."

"Have I got a news flash for you, buddy. Marriage has nothing to do with reproduction. All it takes is a willing male, and the one predictable thing about men is that they're always willing."

Robert's eyes shone with anger. "If I were you, I'd quit talking in terms of timeworn clichés, or I might be tempted to drag out the one about dumb blondes."

"Resist the temptation, and I'll help you check out the generator in the barn." She moved to one side of the step as he passed dangerously close to her, then followed him back upstairs.

"There's no reason for you to come along," he said as he slipped into his thick parka. "I can do it myself."

"I wouldn't dream of not helping." She gave him an innocent smile. While she was relatively certain that her uncle would have hidden the paintings in the house, she wanted to check the barn herself before she left Robert alone out there.

"If you insist. Bring the tool chest, and I'll get the gas out of the truck." He was through the front door before she could demand that he wait for her.

Poor Robert, Miranda thought; she hurriedly slipped into her short leather coat and followed him outside. He was finding being a burglar no easy going. She caught up with him at his truck, where he was in the process of lifting out a huge can of gas.

A blast of snow-clogged air froze the top layer of her skin, and she shuddered convulsively.

Robert glared at her. "Are you cold?"

"Am I cold? You mean just because I'm standing around in sixteen-degree weather, being buffeted by a fifty-mile-an-hour wind?"

"Don't exaggerate." He set the can of gas upon the snow and reached back for a second one. "The wind can't be more than fifteen. Tops."

"I think bottom might be closer," she grumbled, stamping her feet in hope that it would warm them. It didn't.

"You could try dressing appropriately."

"This is appropriate for New York City."

"I hesitate to point out the obvious, but this isn't New York City." So why didn't she buy a warm coat? he wondered. Couldn't she afford to? She'd claimed she owned half of that catering business, but one thing he'd learned early on was not to believe everything a woman said. And even if she had been telling him the truth, the business could be head over heels in debt. Miranda could well be broke, which would account for her eagerness to get her hands on the stolen art. Selling it on the black market would definitely improve her financial position. By exactly how much would depend on what the art was. He sucked in his breath in annoyance; he still lacked any real information about either Miranda or the art. He wished Axel would hurry up with his investigation. Knowing a few facts would make it much easier to deal with the situation. Although— he shot a quick sideways glance at her vivid features— he had the unsettling feeling that Miranda Sheffield would never be an easy person to handle, no matter how much he knew about her.

"Are you frozen to that spot or are you just in a trance?" Miranda's tart words recalled him.

"Don't nag, or you'll never find a man to sire those future generations of Sheffields you're blathering about." He started toward the barn, automatically slowing his brisk stride to match her more tentative steps.

Robert used his shoulder to push the decrepit barn door open and stepped inside. He set the gas cans down in the middle of the dirt floor and, pulling a flashlight out of his coat pocket, swept the area with it.

Miranda blinked as her eyes adjusted to the dim light. Even though they were out of the wind, it seemed colder in here than outside.

"Aha!" Robert's beam of light picked up the thick black wire on the north wall of the barn. He reached for the tool chest she was carrying and set it down beside a rectangular box about four feet square.

"Is that the generator?" She eyed it dubiously. "It's not very big."

"How big does it have to be? All it powers are your lights. Everything else runs on bottled gas."

"I'm aware of that," she said with dignity. "I spent the morning getting everything working."

"If you'd sell out to me, you could go back to New York City, where the electricity comes from the power company."

"I don't want to," she said in perfect truth. New York City held her ex-husband, his new wife and a host of friends and co-workers, all of whom were aware of

Jim's humiliating rejection. And there was the problem of how to convince Jim to sell his half of the business to her. Here all she had to worry about was that Robert would get to the paintings before she did.

She watched Robert wedge himself between the back of the generator and the rough-hewn walls of the barn. She'd never met anyone even vaguely approaching Robert for sheer masculinity, sexual charisma or for attractiveness....

"Stop daydreaming and hand me that long screwdriver," he ordered.

But he fell short in the patience department, she thought wryly as she handed him the tool.

After fifteen minutes of passing tools at his command, Miranda was beginning to feel like an operating nurse out of a grade B movie. Her sense of humor was one of the few things she could still feel. Her fingers tingled with the cold, and she'd lost all contact with her feet five minutes ago.

"I'm almost... Damn!" he muttered. "I can't quite..."

"What's wrong?" Miranda asked.

"I haven't got three hands."

"*No!*" Miranda gave him a look of wide-eyed wonder. "And you've just discovered the fact?"

"Never bite the hand that's helping you," he grumbled.

Miranda laughed. "Which of the three might that be?"

"This is the Adirondacks, not the Poconos. We don't have a comedy circuit here."

"Oh, I don't know." She blew ineffectively upon her fingers. "If you're into black humor, this place is a natural."

"Quit complaining and scoot in here and help me."

"Since you ask so nicely." She scrunched into the space next to him. "What exactly is it you want me to do?"

"Hold that loose wire while I reattach it."

Miranda took a deep breath and leaned across his body to grasp the dangling wire. The icy chill of his nylon parka touched her cheek; she could feel the hard wall of his chest against her shoulder. The very faint scent of his after-shave drifted into her frozen lungs, partially thawing them. He shifted slightly to reach for a tool he'd set on the top of the generator, and Miranda absorbed the feel of his movement.

"Hold that wire steady," Robert ordered.

"Sorry, I'm just cold," Miranda excused herself, hoping he didn't suspect that she was finding his physical presence much more disturbing than the temperature.

Robert glanced at her. "Poor little hothouse flower." His breath warmed her cheek.

"I am not a hothouse flower!" she protested. "But neither am I a snowdrop."

Robert studied her features for a long moment. "No, you're definitely not a snowdrop. You're more like a tiger lily," he finally said.

"Tiger lily?" Miranda made a valiant effort to keep her voice steady. "Tiger lilies are orange and fiery. I'm a cool, Nordic blonde." She shivered. "In fact, I'm a frigid Nordic blonde."

"Are you?" His husky whisper sent a second wave of shivers down her spine, shivers that had nothing to do with the temperature.

"Am I what?" she asked, distracted now by the firm line of his lips as they formed the words.

"Frigid?" He moved his head slightly; his mouth brushed against hers with a whispery softness that made her yearn to deepen the pressure—and hopefully, the sensation. The tip of his tongue touched her bottom lip, sending a jolt through her. Miranda jerked, for one brief moment thinking they'd been shocked by the generator, but the sudden flare in his eyes told her what had really caused it. Robert had obviously felt at least some of what she had. Maybe she shouldn't wait until she returned to New York City to begin trying to relate to men. Maybe she should start right here.

Mesmerized, she watched him reach around her and twist something around the wire. He grunted in satisfaction. "There, that ought to do it."

Miranda hastily scrambled off his chest and stood up, making a production of brushing clinging bits of straw from her jeans while she regained her composure.

"Stand back while I fill it with gas," he ordered.

Miranda obeyed, wrinkling her nose at the smell of gasoline in the enclosed space. Robert finished, then flipped a switch on the side of the generator. To Miranda's relief, it instantly purred to life.

"Let's go in the house and make sure the electricity is working there." Robert gathered up his tool chest and the empty gas can. The other can he set to one side, well away from the generator.

"Aha!" he exclaimed in satisfaction when they emerged from the barn and saw the soft glow of lights through the house's windows.

Robert put the empty gas can and his tool chest into the back of his truck, then followed Miranda into the house.

"I never realized just how beautiful a sixty-watt bulb was." Miranda sighed in satisfaction and closed the front door behind them. "Thank you for your help." She slipped off her coat and tossed it onto the chair by the door. "May I get you a cup of coffee?"

"Thanks, but I don't have time. We're shorthanded today, and I promised Maud I'd get back by four, so she can leave on time." She saw him glance at her reddened hands. Reaching out, he captured them between his much warmer ones and slowly began to rub her fingers.

Miranda stared down. The rhythmic movement of his hands was having a hypnotic effect on her—blocking out everything else—filling her mind with the warmth he was bringing to her fingers.

She wanted to savor every nuance of his touch. The musky scent of his cologne sent out elusive tendrils, enticing her closer, ever closer. She lifted her head and stared into his eyes. Encouraged by the raw desire she saw reflected there, she swayed toward him in an unspoken invitation.

Robert's hands closed around her shoulders, and he pulled her toward him. Miranda continued to stare into his face, fascinated. Somehow his features seemed sharper, more prominent now. His hands urged her closer still, and she sucked in her breath as her breasts came into contact with his chest.

Robert cupped her face in his hands and gazed at her as if uncertain about something. "Beautiful, beautiful Miranda," he murmured. The husky sound of his voice sent tremors over her skin. His thumbs slowly rubbed back and forth across her cheeks, but far from finding the movement soothing, it made her restless. She wanted more, much more.

He lowered his head and once again brushed his lips against hers, but the contact was insubstantial and totally frustrating. Miranda moaned softly and his hand slipped behind her head, spearing her curls to hold her captive. His mouth hardened and his tongue boldly stroked her lips, this time demanding entry. Miranda complied with his unspoken wish and his tongue surged inside. He tasted of coffee and something much more elusive. Something dark and primitively male that had been missing from her life before. The shock of the realization made her lift her head—to find Robert studying her with a narrow-eyed intensity that gave her pause.

Robert watched the dazed look in her eyes fade and wondered if it had been real or assumed solely for his benefit. Could she be good enough to have faked the response he'd just felt? Inga had fooled him—so what did Miranda want? His help in finding the missing art? Or was the kiss to throw him off guard?

Forcing down his dark memories, he said, "Don't forget to come by tomorrow and give Mrs. Kolcheck her demonstration."

Miranda nodded, feeling intense relief at his prosaic words. She simply wanted to enjoy what they'd just shared. She didn't want to start analyzing it. She'd done too much of that recently.

"Take care." He casually flicked the end of her nose with his finger and left.

Miranda watched from behind the faded curtains as he walked briskly down the porch steps and across the yard to his truck. His engine roared to life with a promptness that she wished her own car would emulate. Within seconds he had disappeared into the line of pine trees that bordered the road to the lodge.

Robert Deverill would be a perfect specimen to practice on, she told herself, refusing to even acknowledge, let alone examine, her doubts about the wisdom of beginning her life as a liberated, modern woman with such a worldly man. His sophistication was an advantage, she assured herself. With his experience he wouldn't mistake her interest for anything serious. Not that a man like Robert Deverill was likely to be seriously interested in someone like her. The idea unexpectedly saddened her, and Miranda determinedly turned away from the window. There was no time for her to be standing around, daydreaming. Now that the house was clean and she had electricity, she intended to go through every single drawer, shelf and closet. It wouldn't take long. Her gaze swung around the small living room. She doubted if the entire house had more than six hundred square feet in it.

BY THE FOLLOWING MORNING she had searched every single foot of it. She had found an incredible collection of memorabilia, some of it dating back to the War of 1812, as well as boxes and boxes of what appeared to be plain junk. But to her disappointment, the nearest thing to art she'd found was a deck of tattered playing cards whose backs were decorated with Kentucky Derby winners.

Miranda tossed the deck into the box of things to be disposed of later and sank onto the sofa. She stuck out her tongue at the faded picture of Henry in his army uniform that hung on the wall above the rolltop desk.

"You old reprobate. Where did you hide those paintings?" The picture merely glowered back at her.

"Honestly," she muttered, "I know most families have a black sheep or two, but don't you think you're pushing things? I—" She yelped in surprise when a small gray mouse suddenly ran across her dusty sneaker.

"Oh, great," she went on. "The paintings that I have to find, I can't, and the mice I don't want to find, I'm tripping over.

"And you're starting to talk to yourself," she added. The next step would probably be a padded cell. *I wonder if they'll let me bring the mice for company,* she thought in resignation.

She glanced at the small clock on the desk. Twelve-fifteen. They'd be serving lunch at the inn, but in another hour Mrs. Kolcheck should be able to leave the stragglers to her assistant.

And even if Mrs. Kolcheck was busy, there would be other people at the inn. And noise. She glanced around the room, shivering slightly. She'd never before realized that silence could be so intimidating. So encroaching. As if it were a physical entity, waiting to pounce upon the unwary. And Robert would be there. The intoxicating thought brought her to her feet.

Shortly after one, Miranda pulled into one of the few vacant spaces at the very end of the parking lot and regretfully climbed out of her toasty-warm car. The frigid wind took her breath away. She bent her head and slowly trudged up the gentle incline to the lodge.

"Why, hello there! You look half-frozen," a strange male voice, oozing solicitude, observed. Its owner held the door open for her. "How about if I buy you a hot drink?" He lowered his voice slightly, imbuing it with all kinds of unspoken suggestions.

Miranda blinked rapidly while her eyes struggled to adjust to the dimmer light of the lobby after the glare of the snow. Her vision finally cleared enough for her to take in the truly magnificent physique of the young man in front of her. She stared curiously at him, probing to see if she felt any reaction. She could discover nothing but faint amusement at his well-worn approach. Why would this gorgeous physical specimen leave her cold, while Robert merely had to look at her and her heartbeat accelerated? she asked herself, puzzled. It simply didn't make any sense.

The man, apparently believing that her absorbed silence was due to awe, leaned toward her and whispered intimately, "What can I get you?"

Unexpectedly her sense of humor sparked to life and she gave him a beaming smile. "How kind of you to offer to help. It's so hard to cart all the twins' equipment in. If you could just give me a hand with the playpen, then I'll get—"

"Twins!" His mouth dropped open. "You have twins?"

"Eight months old." Her smile widened at his stunned expression.

"Mmm, lady . . ." The man gulped audibly. "I didn't realize that it was quite so late. I promised my friend I'd meet him on the slopes." He sidled around Miranda and scurried off.

Miranda chuckled and watched him go. Maybe that would teach him to use a little more finesse when he tried to pick up a woman next time. She turned and bumped into someone hard and masculine. The wool of his thick sweater brushed her face, and the tantalizingly familiar scent of his cologne teased her nostrils. His hands closed around her upper arms, holding her steady. She tilted her head and found herself staring into Robert's narrowed eyes. Miranda felt a spurt of pleasure that vaguely shocked her. She wasn't used to feeling this kind of anticipation around a man.

Robert saw the sparkle in her eyes and wondered what had put it there. That young kid's obvious admiration or himself? His gaze wandered down her body and he grimaced in exasperation as he saw her surreptitiously rubbing her chilled hands together.

Why didn't she dress properly? The weather up here was brutal in the winter, and she certainly didn't have much body fat to provide any natural insulation. His eyes dropped to her slender thighs and he felt a sudden tightening in his loins. And that jacket of hers . . . He fought to keep his mind focused on her unsuitable clothing, though all he really wanted to do was to strip it off her delectable body.

"You look like you're about to take an evening stroll down Fifth Avenue." His frustration was almost audible, he realized.

"Don't be ridiculous. No one strolls New York City's streets after dark. They—" She broke off, suddenly noticing the shop behind him. Rows of coats were visible through the window. She stepped around him to get a better look.

"What's the matter?" He turned to see what had caught her eye.

"I'm about to gratify your desire," she said happily.

Robert tensed; an image of her lying naked on his bed popped into his mind.

"And buy a warm parka," she added, a little confused by the glazed look in his eyes. What was the matter with him?

Robert had opened his mouth to say something, anything to prevent her from realizing the effect she was having on him, when Maud rushed up to them.

"Good afternoon, Ms. Sheffield," she said to Miranda. "Robert, it's Axel again. He said to tell you it's urgent and he doesn't have much time."

At last, Robert thought in satisfaction. With any luck at all Axel would have a preliminary report on Miranda's background.

"Thanks, Maud. Excuse me a moment, Miranda. This won't take long."

"I'll wait for you before I start the demonstration," Miranda called after him. Was this some kind of ploy to sneak over to the farmhouse and search it while she was busy in his kitchen with Mrs. Kolcheck? If it really was Axel, where was he calling from? Germany? And what did he have to say that was urgent? Was it about the paintings? Damn! She grimaced and made her way into the shop. If only *she* knew how much *they* knew.

Robert hurried down the short hallway behind the registration desk.

Carefully closing the thick office door behind him, he sank into his leather desk chair and picked up the phone.

"I've got it, Maud," he said. As soon as he heard the click of her hanging up, he demanded, "What did you manage to find out?"

"And a good day to you too, Cousin."

"Facts now, amenities later. Does Miranda really own half of that place?"

"Felker and Felker. Not only owns half, but according to my sources, her talent is the reason it's so successful."

"Really?" Robert was surprised. In his experience, women who looked like Miranda came in and skimmed off the profits from a business some gullible man had built up. They didn't do the work themselves.

"Not only that, but until four months ago she was Mrs. Felker. According to the office gossip my investigator tapped into, Felker had something going on the side with some kid still in her teens. He married her the day the divorce became final."

"He's crazy!" Robert said. "I don't care if the kid he found was a second cousin to Lolita, she couldn't have held a candle to Miranda."

"You wouldn't be getting involved with the ex-Mrs. Felker, would you? Might I remind you that that woman is after our national treasures? I'll guarantee you she doesn't want to display them on her coffee table."

"I didn't say she was an ethical woman, just that she's a gorgeous one. Although your information does raise the question of why she would want the art, if she already owns half a successful business."

"Maybe to buy out her ex-husband's half? Maybe to catch herself a second husband? Maybe she just wants some financial security? Who knows what goes on in another person's mind? Just remember that we have to find our heritage first."

"I'm perfectly aware of that," Robert said impatiently. "And I'm looking every chance I get. Tell me, since you're so free with the advice, have you managed to get a line on exactly what it is I'm looking for?"

"No, but I have gotten a lead on Henry's movements, right before he was shipped home. We're getting close. I can feel it."

Robert grimaced. He felt things, too, when he was around Miranda, but was sure they weren't the kind of things Axel was talking about.

"If only I could get back to help you." Axel's frustration was audible. "But these contract negotiations are going so slowly and—"

"Don't worry, Axel. I can handle the situation here, at least for the time being. But I would appreciate anything else you can find out about Miranda. You can forget her ex-husband. He's obviously dealing from a short deck."

Axel laughed. "Why don't you just marry her? I could search the house on your honeymoon."

"You know my views on marriage." Robert's words were spoken all the more emphatically, because for one wild second he'd been tempted by the image Axel's teasing words had suggested. "After what Philip went through when he married that little gold digger he thought he was in love with...."

"Philip was a weak, ineffectual man," Axel said flatly. "Instead of getting drunk and wrapping his car around a tree, he should have kicked her out and gotten on with his life."

"He loved her," Robert said harshly, remembering the pain in his friend's face all those years ago when Philip had agonized over his wife's many infidelities.

"No, Philip loved what he wanted her to be."

"But—"

"And if you hadn't been barely eighteen at the time, and a rather sheltered eighteen at that, you would have been able to see it. Not that it matters anymore. Philip's dead. Let him rest in peace. I've got to go. I'll get back to you when I can."

"Good luck on the contract," Robert said absently; he hung up, his mind still on Axel's words. Was Axel right? Had Philip been weak? Robert hadn't thought so at the time. He'd thought that the twenty-four-year-old Philip was the last word in sophistication. He'd been flattered when Philip had admired his tennis game, because Philip was already a well-known name in the tennis world.

Philip had been Robert's first real friend on the tennis circuit and he had taken that friendship seriously. He had suffered through Philip's pain at his failing marriage as if it had been his own. Philip had said he was helpless to do anything because he was in love with his wife. But was that really why he hadn't done anything? For the first time Robert examined his friend's motives with the eyes of experience. He sighed. There might be something to Axel's contention.

Uncomfortable at the thought, he pushed back his chair and got to his feet. Whatever Philip had felt for his wife, he should never have married her. Grandfather had been right. Marriage entailed a whole lot more than a rush of hormones. Marriage was for the long haul, and for that you needed mutual interests and business and family ties. That was what made a successful marriage. Not sexual attraction, potent as it could be. Not Miranda.

5

"GOOD AFTERNOON," Miranda offered, keeping a wary eye on the knife Mrs. Kolcheck was wielding.

"It hasn't been so far," Mrs. Kolcheck grumbled. "My supplier was late, the salad girl quit, and now you're here."

Miranda grinned at her. "See, your luck is changing."

Mrs. Kolcheck reluctantly smiled back. "I suppose you might as well come in and get this over with."

Miranda reminded herself of the electricity she now enjoyed, thanks to Robert's help, and came in. Her sense of honor demanded that she try to keep her part of the bargain. She didn't want Robert to think she was one of those people who took but never gave. Although his own motives certainly didn't bear too close a scrutiny, she thought with an apprehensive shiver. Not that she couldn't handle him in their race for the paintings. It was his ties to Axel and the German government that worried her the most.

She also wanted to find out what Mrs. Kolcheck knew about her uncle and his relationship with Robert. Anything that might give her a clue as to where the paintings were hidden.

"You wouldn't know anything about salads, would you?" Mrs. Kolcheck gestured with the knife and Miranda winced, hoping that the woman didn't lose her grip on the handle. If she did, Miranda could wind up as a shish kebab.

"Nope," Miranda lied.

"Wanna learn?" Mrs. Kolcheck persisted.

"Nope," Miranda repeated.

"You ain't planning on staying around?"

"It's not that, exactly. It's just that my plans are rather fluid at the moment."

Mrs. Kolcheck stared at her. "You mean you drink?"

"Not so far."

"Jobs are scarce up here, you know." Mrs. Kolcheck apparently refused to take no for an answer.

"The problem, Mrs. Kolcheck, is that I'm a pastry chef. I haven't done any cooking such as you do since college."

"College!" Mrs. Kolcheck cackled. "You mean to tell me that you went to college to learn how to cook?"

"Among other things. Oh, and before I forget, I want to thank you for sending all those dinners over to my uncle," Miranda said with seeming casualness. "It was very kind of you."

"Wasn't really my kindness. Mr. Deverill said to do it."

"Why was that?" Miranda asked, remembering that Robert had said something about an agreement he'd had with her uncle.

Mrs. Kolcheck pursed her lips, considering. "Don't know for a fact. Could be he was buttering him up."

"Oh?"

"Maybe Mr. Deverill thought the old geezer'd leave him the farm when he died." She shook her head. "I could of told him that it'd never work. Blood always wins in the end."

"It does?"

"Sure. You inherited, didn't you? And you never did a thing for the old man."

"No, I guess I didn't," Miranda admitted, feeling guilty, even though her common sense told her that there wasn't much she could have done. In a very real sense, her parents' divorce had irrevocably split the family. Henry had been her father's uncle, and even though Miranda had continued to write to him, he had never asked her to visit, and her pride had never allowed her to come without an invitation.

"'Course you ought to feel lucky, 'cause you weren't the old guy's only relative," Mrs. Kolcheck continued. "At least, not according to Dave. About three months ago, he went over there with Henry's supper and found him out on his porch, yelling at some man parked in the driveway. Dave said that Old Henry was so mad, he was like to pop a blood vessel. Said he kept yelling that the man wasn't no nephew of his. Hadn't been since the day he ditched his family to run off with that . . ." Mrs. Kolcheck lowered her voice and glanced toward the other end of the huge kitchen, where several people were working. "Whore. Old Henry said that he needn't think he was going to bring her and her damned passel of brats to his place for a free vacation."

"Really?" Miranda's eyes widened in surprise. She'd always known that Henry had been mad about her parents' divorce, but hadn't realized he'd been that mad.

"Yup!" Mrs. Kolcheck seemed gratified at Miranda's reaction. "Dave said that Old Henry waved a rifle at the man. Told him to get off his property, before he put him six feet under with the other sinners."

Miranda stifled a grin. Her father would have hated being made to look foolish.

At least she didn't have to worry about her father finding out about the paintings. Miranda mentally checked him off her list of possible contenders. He hadn't known about them before the divorce and couldn't have found out about them afterward, since Henry hadn't even allowed him onto the property.

"Now you'd better get on with your demonstration, 'cause that salad girl taking off with her boyfriend has put me behind. Just you remember, nothing too fancy."

"I'll remember." Miranda walked to the gleaming, stainless steel sinks and washed her hands.

"So there you are." Robert's voice jerked her head around as effectively as if he'd pulled a string. Savoring the quick surge of exhilaration she felt at the sight of him, she dried her hands. She was still surprised that she could derive so much enjoyment from just looking at him. Out of the corner of her eye she saw him perch upon a stool and lean toward her, as if waiting to be entertained.

Reminding herself that modern, sophisticated women didn't drool over men, even ones that looked like Robert Deverill, she spoke directly to Mrs. Kolcheck. "I thought we'd start with a New York-type cheesecake, a chocolate mousse and a low-cholesterol lemon chiffon."

"Low cholesterol!" Mrs. Kolcheck hooted. "Whatever for? Most everybody that comes in here is in their twenties and thirties. Cholesterol is an old folks' worry."

"I think you'll find that a lot of young folks are worrying about it, too, so that they won't have to worry about heart attacks when they get older," Miranda said mildly.

"But—" Mrs. Kolcheck began.

"You probably haven't paid much attention to the problem because you're a woman," Robert threw in. "I read somewhere that some study or other suggests that women might have a built-in immunity to the worst ef-

fects of high cholesterol. At least until after meno-
pause."

"Now see here!" Mrs. Kolcheck's gaunt cheeks turned
beet red. "We'll have none of that kind of dirty talk in
my kitchen!"

"Yeah." Miranda tried hard to suppress her laughter
at Robert's dumbfounded expression. "You watch your
tongue."

"He probably just wasn't thinking," Mrs. Kolcheck
explained. "Normally he acts like a decent man."

"That's a relief to know." Miranda gave him an innocent look. "For a second there I was worried."

"If the two of you don't stop discussing my morals,
I'll give you something to really be worried about," he
grumbled.

"Oh, but it wasn't your morals that had us worried." Miranda grinned unrepentantly. "It was your
lack of them."

"Mmm...yes...about those recipes?" Mrs. Kolcheck suddenly seemed to remember that Robert was
her boss.

"Certainly." Miranda began her demonstration.

An hour and a half later, she put the cheesecake into
the oven and stretched tiredly. She turned, then felt a
flush of excitement stain her cheeks as she noticed how
Robert's eyes narrowed, no doubt at the sight of her
breasts outlined against the thin cotton of her blouse.
She felt a surge of pleasure. For the first time in her life

she experienced a sense of power at being a woman. A power she wasn't totally comfortable with. She and Jim had related more mentally than physically, she realized suddenly.

"You think those chiffons you made will be ready for tonight?" Mrs. Kolcheck asked and Miranda turned to her.

"Sure. Another hour in the refrigerator and they'll be fine. So will the mousses, but don't try to serve the cheesecake today. It needs to set overnight."

"I'll remember, and any afternoon you get lonely over at that farm of yours, you feel free to come visit me," Mrs. Kolcheck offered.

"Thank you." Miranda glanced at Robert, who was meticulously licking the cheesecake mixing bowl, to see how he'd reacted to the invitation. He hadn't. Could it be because he'd told Mrs. Kolcheck to ask her? In order to get her away from the farm, so he could search the house for the paintings? Was she becoming paranoid?

Robert took one last lick from the bowl and stood up. "Why don't you get yourself a cup of coffee and come into my office? I have a couple of things I want to ask you about all this."

"Sure." She poured herself a cup of coffee and followed him out of the kitchens.

His office exuded a warmth that invited a visitor to curl up in one of the burgundy, leather wing chairs in front of the crackling fire in the fieldstone fireplace.

"Very nice." Her gaze swept over the huge mahogany desk, across the multicolored Tabriz carpet to linger on the picture window, which gave him an unobstructed view of the mountains. "Very nice, indeed."

"Thank you." Robert motioned her toward one of the chairs and sat down across from her.

All he needed was a pipe and a faithful dog at his feet and he'd look like the perfect country squire, Miranda thought. No, not just a simple country squire, she amended as she surreptitiously studied him through the rising steam of her coffee. With his air of command and rugged good looks, he should be royalty. She tried to picture him as Bonnie Prince Charlie, brandishing a broadsword.

"I wanted to ask you where you order your supplies from." His question dissolved the delightful image, and she forced herself to concentrate on the present.

"Supplies?" she repeated.

"The specialized items, like the molds you suggested for the lemon chiffon and the parfait glasses for the mousse. How big an order do you have to place to get a quantity discount, and do you get a discount for payment within thirty days?"

Miranda opened her mouth to answer, then closed it when she realized she didn't know. Jim had always handled that end of the business. As long as the equipment and supplies she'd wanted had appeared when she'd wanted them, she hadn't worried. But that ignorance was a luxury she would not be able to afford in the future, she realized with a sinking heart. When she went into business on her own, she was going to have to devote a lot of time to the financial end of catering.

"I don't know what the things cost," she admitted.

"Well, where do you buy your equipment?"

Miranda shrugged. "My ex-husband took care of all the details," she told him; the familiar bitter, frustrated pain filled her once again.

"And you're still in business together?" Robert probed.

"Not for long. The present situation is not working out," she said, carefully understating the case.

"It usually doesn't when that first mad rush of sensual desire fades," Robert agreed.

Mad, sensual desire? His words echoed in her mind. Mad...sensual...awareness.... She slowed them down and examined them, feeling confused. She and Jim had never shared anything even vaguely approaching a mad, sensual awareness. Was that why he had succumbed so swiftly to Brandy's charms?

"So now you're going to dissolve the partnership," Robert continued. "Did you make any provisions for it happening when you first set it up?"

Miranda grimaced. "Of course not. I didn't go into the marriage expecting it to end in divorce."

"That's going to make it tricky. One of you is going to have to start over."

"Not me! I've already given Brandy my husband. She isn't going to get my business, too!" Miranda winced as she heard the strident sound of her own voice. "I'm sorry," she muttered. "I didn't mean to sound so . . ."

"Human? Of course you're mad. He screwed up your safe little world and now he's trying to kick you out of it altogether."

"Mad?" Miranda stared at Robert in shock. He was right. She wasn't heartbroken at Jim's defection, she was mad. Furiously, blazingly angry.

"You're right. I am mad, and what's more, I'm going to get even," she said defiantly.

"I've been told that the best revenge is living well."

"You don't understand." She gestured vaguely. "It's like . . . like Jim told me that I was an inferior product and he wanted to trade me in. Think how you'd feel if you had a wife who came home one day and said she'd found someone she liked better."

Robert felt his face harden; he remembered the pain on Philip's face as he'd recounted his wife's latest sexual exploit. "It happens all the time in the world I used to inhabit. Usually about the time the woman had run through the poor sucker's money."

"Oh?" Miranda was taken aback.

"That's why when I marry, love will be far down on my list of requirements. Having common interests and values lasts much longer."

"Almost ten years."

"What?"

"It lasted almost ten years," she repeated. "That's the kind of marriage Jim and I had, and I don't think it made it any easier when it ended. I still feel rejected. As if I had nothing of value to offer a man."

Robert stared blankly at her and considered what she was saying. Was she right? In her case, common interests hadn't insured a lasting marriage. Nor, from the sound of it, a particularly happy one. But things had been different with his grandparents. They'd been married almost thirty-five years before his grandmother had died. That had been a happy marriage. His grandfather had told him so. But what would his grandmother have told him? He tried to remember one spontaneous physical gesture between them. He couldn't. They'd treated each other with a formal politeness that could have hidden any emotion, all the way from hatred to intense joy. Had his grandparents been truly happy, or had they settled for contentment? One thing was sure, though. His grandfather's recipe for a successful marriage wasn't infallible. It hadn't worked for Miranda.

He felt an unexpected urge to comfort her. "Tell me, Miranda. If you were hired to provide treats for a bunch of three-year-olds at a party, would you send caviar and champagne?"

She frowned. "Of course not. I'd send hot dogs and chocolate cake. But what does that have to do with anything?"

He walked toward her, succumbing to his growing compulsion to touch her. "Because from the sound of things, your ex-husband was a man who couldn't see beyond hot dogs. And you, my dear, definitely come under the heading of caviar. Or, perhaps, fine brandy," he murmured, "because kissing you is potent enough."

He perched on the arm of her chair, his hard thigh pressed against her arm; her pulse skittered. Trying to appear nonchalant, she tilted her head and studied him. His lips were lifted in a sensual smile and his eyes were narrowed. Tiny lines radiated from the corners. His eyes had a greenish glitter that made her stomach lurch in anticipation.

Miranda leaned toward him provocatively, increasing the pressure on her arm. She could feel the movement of his muscles when he shifted slightly, and caught her breath as his forefinger traced the bridge of her nose.

"You have such soft skin," he murmured. "Soft and infinitely touchable." He lowered his head. His warm breath wafted across her cheek, a second before his lips met hers, moving lightly over them.

Miranda's heartbeat accelerated and she grasped the back of his neck, trying to pull him closer. To her frustration, he didn't immediately deepen the kiss. He seemed content to learn the shape, taste and texture of her lips. It was a contentment she didn't share. The emotions he raised were so new that she wanted to wring every last drop of sensation out of them for fear they might never be felt again.

"Robert!" Maud called through the closed door. "Could you please come out to the desk? Some guy who canceled his reservations last week has just shown up. He says he changed his mind and didn't think we would have rebooked his room. Unfortunately he was wrong."

"Damn!" Robert reluctantly got to his feet. "There are times when I wish I were back on the tennis circuit. You have no idea what some of my so-called customers can be like."

"You've got to be kidding!" Miranda swallowed her disappointment at the interruption and followed him out of his office. "I work in catering, remember. We had one customer who changed her mind eight times before she finally settled on the main course. And another one who called the morning of the wedding and wanted me to redesign the cake because of some dream she'd had the night before." Not that she'd been the one who'd had to deal with either customer, Miranda remembered. Jim had been the one who'd coped with them. Her role had been to supervise the kitchens.

Robert remained as he listened to the upset guest. Still thoughtful, Miranda collected her coat from the kitchen and left. It took a lot of patience and tact to deal with the public. It also took skill. Skill that she had never bothered to acquire, because there had been no need. But there'd be lots of need if she bought Jim out. She would be the one on the front lines.

Moving carefully, she crossed the well-sanded parking lot to her car. Even if she hired an office manager, a lot of the final decisions would have to be hers. Just as Maud had come for Robert to resolve a sticky situation, her employees would come to her.

Miranda unlocked her car and climbed in. The only alternative would be for her to work for someone else, and that was not an idea that appealed to her at all. She'd been her own boss for far too long to ever be happy having to do things someone else's way.

Miranda worried over the problem all the way to the farm, where she faced her overriding concern. The paintings. She decided to check out the basement that evening. It took all evening to sort through the boxes of canning jars, tools and just plain junk that her uncle had accumulated over his lifetime. The only thing she found of interest was a fascinating collection of old cooking utensils.

At least she was able to rule out the basement as a hiding place, she consoled herself late that night, tiredly collapsing into bed.

IN THE MORNING, when she started to fix breakfast, she realized she'd almost used up the food that Robert had given her. Since the sky was clear and it hadn't snowed overnight, she decided to take advantage of the relatively mild weather to go into town and shop.

Before she left, she posted a note on her front door, saying she'd be back momentarily. Hopefully, if Robert did sneak over in her absence, he wouldn't try to search the house, for fear of getting caught in the act. She grimaced. Fear of discovery didn't seem to have slowed him down so far. He had to know that her options, even if she caught him red-handed, were extremely limited. She could hardly call the police and accuse him of trying to resteal her stolen paintings.

Miranda sighed dispiritedly. There was a whole lot more to crime than she'd ever thought.

She had discovered one thing; she was not cut out to be a hermit. She needed daily interaction with people.

It didn't take her long to complete her shopping, for the simple reason that there wasn't that much to select from. The village's shopping facilities consisted of a small strip mall, which included a grocery store, a hardware store, two taverns and a drugstore.

Loath to return to the isolation of the farm, and feeling it was much too early to go over to the lodge under any pretext, she decided to go into the drugstore and see if they had any paperback books for sale. She was wandering toward the back of the store when a display near the pharmacy counter caught her eye.

Casting a furtive glance around to make sure no one was watching her, she walked over to study it. When she'd originally started sharpening her basic feminine skills on Robert, her goal had been to learn to feel comfortable with the sophisticated sexual teasing he'd employed with her. And she'd wanted to kiss him, she added honestly.

Now that wasn't enough. Like a child suddenly turned loose in a candy shop, she wanted it all. She wanted to make love with him, wanted to explore what she was capable of feeling. The fact that she didn't trust him an inch when it came to the paintings didn't change how she felt. Her emotions had a logic all of their own.

For a brief second she considered the idea that her reaction to Robert might be fueled by her ex-husband's rejection, but refused to worry about it. She was a mature, adult woman, and if she wanted to have an affair, she would. So she would have to take responsibility for her actions.

Uncertain what to do, she gnawed on her lower lip. The problem was that she'd had no experience with the ins and outs of birth control. When she hadn't gotten pregnant after four years of marriage, she and Jim had gone in for tests. Tests that had unexpectedly revealed that Jim was sterile. Probably as a result of a nasty case of mumps he'd somehow contracted during his sophomore year of college, the doctor had surmised. But things were different now. Now she needed to protect herself, and the most logical way to do so was to buy one of these boxes of condoms.

Thoughtful, she read the labels—ribbed, unribbed, thin, extrathin, large, extralarge. She frowned. How large was large, and how was she supposed to know which would fit Robert? She could hardly call him up and say, "Oh, and by the way, have you ever measured . . . ?" She flushed at the very idea.

"May I help you, miss?" The elderly pharmacist leaned over the counter.

"Mmm, no thanks," she mumbled. There was no way she was going to get into a discussion on the merits of different types of condoms with a stranger old enough to be her grandfather. She waited until the man had moved away, then hurriedly tossed a random sampling into her shopping cart. She'd study them later in the privacy of her home.

A privacy that didn't appear to have been violated, she concluded when she returned to the farmhouse. The

note she'd written was still there, and there were no new
tire tracks in the snow.

She made short work of unloading the car and after
eating a can of soup, weighed the pros and cons of
tackling the attic.

"There's no use postponing the evil moment, Miranda. You're going to have to go up there sooner or
later. It might as well be sooner," she told herself. The
sound of a human voice, even her own, made her feel
better.

She put on the new parka and hat she'd bought at the
lodge. The attic was unheated and probably wasn't
much warmer than the nineteen degrees it was outside.
Hopefully she would be able to locate the paintings
quickly.

As a hope, it proved futile. Two hours later she was
not only partially frozen but thoroughly frustrated.
She'd searched every trunk, box and bag in the entire
attic, and the only art she'd found was photos of some
of her ancestors.

She glanced around the clutter in exasperation.
Where could Henry have hidden the blasted things? Her
gaze dropped to the rough wooden flooring at her feet.
Could he have rolled the paintings up and shoved them
underneath the floorboards? There was no way of telling without ripping up the floor. She sighed. It could
well come to that.

A banging from downstairs caught her unawares and she froze, straining to hear what it was. The sound came again, this time louder and she swallowed nervously. She looked out the attic's one window, but it faced the back of the property. There was no way for her to see who had driven up. It could be anyone. A guest from the lodge who'd gotten lost, a determined salesman, a serial killer... Her fingers tightened around her flashlight as she tried to decide what to do, besides sign up for a course in self-defense the moment she returned to New York City.

"Miranda?" Robert's voice floated up the stairs. "Where are you?"

Miranda's body sagged in relief. "I'm up in the attic. I'll be down in a second." She hurried toward the stairs. She didn't want him coming up here and realizing that she'd searched it. Although letting him know she was looking for the paintings, too, wasn't a bad idea at this point. Perhaps, in his eagerness to get to them first, he'd tip his hand as to what he knew.

That was the trouble with the whole situation, she thought in exasperation. Everything seemed to hinge on "maybe," "perhaps" or "if." The only thing she knew for certain was that fifteen years ago her uncle had had the paintings in this house. And given her impression that he'd never thrown anything away in his life, they were probably still here.

"Where have you been?" Robert asked.

"In the attic." She savored the rush of pleasure she felt at the sight of him. He was wearing worn jeans that hugged his long legs and a brown leather bomber jacket that made his broad shoulders appear even broader.

"Attic!" He stripped off his jacket and tossed it onto the round, oak table. "Why would you go into an unheated attic in the dead of winter?"

"I was curious about what was in all those trunks," she said, watching him close to see how he responded.

Robert held on to his expression of mild interest with an effort. So Axel was right. She was after the stolen art. The question was, why did she want it? To sell? In the beginning he might have thought so, but now he wasn't so sure. She seemed so straightforward. But then, so had his fiancée. He remembered his youthful gullibility. Inga's melting, blue eyes had seemed completely without guile and her soft, pouting lips so innocently provocative. He'd believed every lying word that had fallen from them. Believed them right up to the day he'd overheard her bragging to a friend about the rich young fool she was dangling on a string.

He grimaced in self-disgust. She'd certainly been right about one thing. He'd been a fool to fall for nothing more than a face and a helpless manner. But he was no longer an impressionable twenty-year-old.

He studied Miranda's watchful expression with a confused feeling that teetered between indulgence and fear. If there was a woman alive who could con him, she was standing not four feet in front of him. Robert pulled his thoughts away from this dangerous territory and tried for lightness instead. "If you're looking for buried treasure, you can forget it. Old Henry kept his money in the bank like any sensible person."

"I know, but perhaps he had something else of value stashed away," she suggested.

"He did," Robert said wryly. "It was the deed to this place. It's worth a great deal to you if you'd sell to me. I'd even be willing to throw in free use of one of the rooms at the lodge for several weeks during the season."

"The problem is that I don't want to sell." Trying one last time to get information, she said, "I was thinking more in terms of antiques he might have collected."

"Henry?" Robert had no trouble looking skeptical now. "As far as I know, he never collected anything. Although . . ." He rubbed his jaw thoughtfully. Miranda could almost feel the rough silk texture of his skin. How would his cheek feel against her breast?

"Although?" she repeated, hearing her voice unexpectedly husky.

"There's all that pink glass in the china closet in the living room," he offered.

"There's more of it in the basement and the attic."

"I could be wrong, but I think it's Depression Glass. My mother has a few pieces and she says it's valuable."

"Really?" Miranda wasn't sure what to think. Why had he seemed uninterested when she told him she was searching the attic? Because he didn't think she was any real competition for the paintings? Or because, despite her hints, he didn't realize that she knew about them? She swallowed a sigh. Still more questions, when what she could really use was a few answers.

6

"WHY ARE YOU in my kitchen, if it isn't too much to ask?" Miranda decided to ask a question she could reasonably expect an answer to.

"I brought you something." Robert moved slightly and gestured toward the brown wicker picnic basket sitting on the kitchen counter behind him. "We sold out of both the chiffon and the mousse last night, so I asked Mrs. Kolcheck to make some more when she came in this morning. I brought you some samples."

"I see," she said slowly, wondering if his trip had been motivated by a desire to see her or to use her culinary skills again. Or had he hoped she'd be gone, so that he could search the house?

"I also brought you some mousetraps." He reached behind the picnic basket and picked up a large paper sack. "I got these from Dave. He says they're the latest thing."

"That's good, because mice have to be the oldest thing." She grimaced. "I set my dinner down on the counter last night and went to the refrigerator to get a can of soda. And when I came back, I found a mouse sitting in the middle of my green beans."

"These should take care of your rodent problem." Robert handed her several triangular containers open at both ends. "You put these things out in here and I'll hide the rest in the living room. And be careful not to touch the inside. It's covered with a powerful glue."

Miranda gingerly accepted the traps and went into the pantry, where she carefully set them behind some of the containers. She hoped they worked. She lived in dread of having one of the little beasties run across her in her sleep.

She went into the living room. A quick glance around was enough to confirm her suspicions. Robert wasn't there. Quietly she crept across the room toward the tiny hallway that led to the bedroom. At first sight the room appeared to be empty, but a muffled thump from the closet caught her attention.

She tiptoed across the threadbare carpet and peered around the half-open closet door—to find Robert rummaging through an antique hatbox. Resisting the impulse to tell him that he was wasting his time, that she'd already searched the closet, she leaned against the door frame and cleared her throat.

He jumped.

"May I help you?" She glanced pointedly at the hatbox.

Robert hastily pulled his hand out of the hatbox, apparently at a loss for an excuse. "I smelled something coming from the box," he offered tentatively.

"A rat, no doubt," she said dryly. "Why don't I finish for you?"

"That's all right. I'm done now. Why don't you pour us some coffee from the thermos in the picnic basket while I wash my hands? Then you can give me your opinion of Mrs. Kolcheck's efforts."

"Sure." Miranda waited until he'd left the room, then followed him out. It wasn't safe to leave him alone anywhere in the house, she thought in resignation as she poured the coffee.

"Thank you." He accepted the cup she handed him. "A strong shot of caffeine is exactly what I need." He took a satisfying swallow of the brew.

"Now, then." He peered into the interior of the basket. "Which would you like to try first, the lemon chiffon?"

"Okay by me." Miranda accepted the dessert cup and spoon he handed her. She took a sample, frowning when the taste registered.

"What's wrong?" he asked.

"It's a little . . . overpowering."

"Are you saying that it's not very good?"

"On the same scale that wars tend to be dangerous to your health," she said tartly. "Have you tasted this . . . this atrocity?"

"I told you. I don't eat sweets."

She grimaced. "So you used me as a guinea pig. I should have remembered what you said about buying the farm from my heirs."

"Maybe it was a onetime fluke. Try the chocolate mousse."

More cautious this time, Miranda took a small spoonful. Her mouth immediately puckered at the bitter taste. She swallowed and grabbed her coffee.

"Now what?" Robert asked in resignation.

"I found out where she got the extra sugar for the chiffon. She took it out of the mousse. She also used unsweetened chocolate instead of sweetened."

Robert looked puzzled. "I don't understand what happened."

Miranda shrugged. "I chose these recipes, because any semicompetent cook should be able to make them."

"You're saying my cook is incompetent?"

"No. I am merely pointing out that she didn't want to cook the desserts in the first place, and when you forced the issue, she managed to mess up two painfully simple recipes. You can draw your own conclusions."

Robert ran his fingers through his hair in frustration. "The trouble is that good cooks really are hard to find. Believe it or not, most people don't want to live up here."

Miranda looked out the window at the seemingly inexhaustible supply of snow on the ground and then at him. "I can't imagine why."

"You have no idea of the problems involved in running the lodge. I need to keep the cook happy."

"Within reason," Miranda agreed, "but limiting your menu because she doesn't want to be bothered is not reasonable. Her job is to cook what the customers want, not what she wants."

"So what am I supposed to do? Get rid of her and let the guests toast hot dogs over an open fire?"

"Have you ever specifically listed what you expect Mrs. Kolcheck to do?"

"Cook," he said succinctly.

"Now there's a nebulous order. Part of your problem would appear to be inefficient management," she said seriously. "People work much better when they know exactly what is expected of them."

"And if the day had twice as many hours in it, then, maybe, just maybe, I'd have time to get to it! I'm only one man!"

"What you need—" She was interrupted by a scuffling sound coming from the pantry.

"What's that?" Robert asked.

Miranda cocked her head to one side and listened. "I'm not sure." She got to her feet and cracked the pantry door, peering in.

"For heaven's sake, go in and look."

"I prefer caution," she said seriously. "Considering Uncle Henry's other eccentricities, I wouldn't be the least surprised to find out that he had a pet boa constrictor lurking around the house."

Robert peered over her shoulder and Miranda could feel his hard body pressing against her from shoulder to thigh. "If Henry had had a boa constrictor, you wouldn't be overrun with mice."

Miranda tried to swallow the dry sensation in her mouth. "Good point. I never thought I'd be grateful to have mice, but small furry things are definitely preferable to long, slimy ones."

"Snakes aren't slimy. They—aha!" He strode into the pantry. More cautiously, Miranda followed.

"Aha, what?" She looked around.

"Aha, a mouse." He reached behind a stack of battered pots and picked up one of the traps she'd set out. Miranda jumped back; a small, gray mouse was dangling from it by its tail.

"Yup," she agreed. "That's a mouse, all right. Now what?"

He looked blankly at her. "What do you mean, now what?"

"You've caught it. Now what do you intend to do with it?"

"Me?" he protested. "It's your mouse."

"But it's your trap," she countered. "You do something."

Robert glanced at the struggling rodent, then looked back at Miranda. "I categorically refuse to kill something this small and defenseless."

Miranda grimaced. "Having tasted Mrs. Kolcheck's desserts, I might have known you'd shrink from any unpleasantness."

"We could put it outside," he offered.

"Outside! It's freezing out there!"

Robert gave her an exasperated look. "What did you expect to do with the mice, once you'd caught them?"

Miranda shrugged. "I didn't think about it. I don't really want to hurt them. I just want them gone."

"Well, we could try putting them up in the loft in the barn. There's plenty of straw up there to keep him warm."

"It's worth a try," Miranda agreed.

"Here, hold him while I get my coat."

Miranda instinctively stepped back. "Just because I don't want to kill it doesn't mean that I want to get friendly with it. Set it down on the floor and we'll both get our coats."

With a grimace, Robert did as she'd suggested and Miranda hurried to get her parka. She kept a cautious distance behind him as he carried the beast to the barn.

Once there, she followed him up the rickety ladder that led to the loft. The faint light filtering through the filthy windows at each end created a surrealistic atmosphere.

"Any ideas on how to get the mouse out of the trap?" Robert asked.

She squinted at the squirming rodent. "Weren't there any directions on the trap?"

"Of course not. You're supposed to do it in. Maybe we could try pushing his tail off the sticky substance with a stick?"

"A stick?" Miranda peered into the gloomy light. "There's one." She plunged her hand into the musty straw and triumphantly handed out a short, fat stick.

Robert kicked aside the thin layer of straw to reveal the battered floorboards. He set the mousetrap down and held it while Miranda used the stick to pry their captive loose.

Finally, with a last shove, the frantic mouse was free. He jumped toward Miranda, who instinctively stepped back. For a second she thought her sense of disorientation was due to her sudden movement, then realized that she wasn't moving. The trapdoor she'd stepped on was.

"Robert!" She frantically grabbed for something to hold on to; an ominous, cracking sound echoed through the funereal silence. There was a momentary sensation of weightlessness, then she was jerked forward, right into Robert's arms.

He cradled her protectively against him, shaken by the speed of events. One minute they'd been bending over the mouse, and the next she'd been disappearing down a hole.

Miranda pressed closer to the warmth and safety of Robert's chest and felt his arms tighten comfortingly around her trembling body.

"I could have been killed," she said unsteadily.

"Hardly. That's a dirt floor down there, and it's only ten feet away. The worst that could have happened would have been that you'd have broken a leg. Or two," he added thoughtfully.

"As long as it was nothing serious," she said dryly.

Gradually the full implications of what had almost happened sank in. "It could have been. If you'd been here by yourself, you could have frozen to death down there before anyone found you."

Miranda shivered at the truth of what he was saying. In this weather, anyone unable to get to cover could quickly freeze.

"I want you to promise me that you'll stay out of the loft unless someone is here with you."

"I'll do better than that," she said. "I'll promise to stay out of the loft, period. There's nothing out here that I want. Unless . . ." She paused. Could Henry have hidden the missing paintings up here? She peered at the roof, measuring the light coming in between the good-sized cracks. This place would leak like a sieve when it rained. And not only that, there are no locks on the doors. No, she decided, Henry wouldn't have hidden the paintings out here. He'd been eccentric, not senile.

"Unless what?" Robert gave her a tiny shake, making her excruciatingly aware of how closely they were standing.

Miranda didn't want to worry about Henry's purloined paintings. She wanted to kiss Robert. To kiss him and keep right on kissing him. In fact, she wanted to do a whole lot more than just kiss him. And she was going to do just that, she decided in a burst of determination. This was as good a time as any to try to push their relationship forward, into another stage. A much more intimate stage. But not out here, where the frigid temperature would discourage anything more than the briefest of kisses. "Oh, just that it suddenly occurred to me that Uncle Henry might have stored some more of that Depression Glass up here," she improvised.

Robert turned to look around the loft. "I doubt it," he finally said. "Henry's arthritis really bothered him the last few years."

"True," Miranda muttered, her mind busy with the more immediate problem of how to seduce Robert without being obvious about it. Someone ought to write a book on the subject for newly liberated women, she thought in frustration. She lifted her hand to straighten her cap, which was now listing over one eye.

"What's that?" He took her hand and studied it. "It's a splinter." He frowned at the offending gray chunk in her palm.

Miranda squinted at it. "Yup, it sure is. Fortunately, I'm so cold I can't feel a thing."

"Let's get back to the house and I'll dig it out for you."

"*Dig* it out?" she repeated. "No one is digging anything out of my body. I will gently remove it myself."

"You can't." He started down the ladder. "It's your right hand."

"I might not be ambidextrous, but I'm not totally helpless," she grumbled as she followed him down. She tensed momentarily when she felt his hands slide under her parka to grasp her waist and steady her. They seemed to burn through her sweater to the receptive skin below.

Miranda swallowed and slowly continued down the last few rungs, deliberately prolonging his hold on her. Much too soon she reached the ground and he removed his hands.

"Do you have any tweezers?" he asked.

Miranda shuddered as they emerged from the protection of the barn and the wind hit them full force. "Of course," she gasped.

"Good. I'll have it out in no time."

Miranda had opened her mouth to repeat that she would do it herself when the possibilities inherent in the situation occurred to her. In order to remove a splinter, he'd have to get close to her. Very close. Without the bulk of their coats between them.

"Thank you, I'd appreciate that," she murmured.

Once in the house, she sat down on the sofa beside Robert and held out the tweezers and her hand.

Robert studied the splinter and tilted his head to one side, as if trying to get a better perspective. Finally he announced, "We need some iodine."

"Iodine stains. I'll douse the wound with rubbing alcohol when you're done. Provided, of course, that you ever do get done," she added pointedly, wishing he'd hurry up. It wasn't all that big a splinter, and she had other things on her mind.

Miranda's eyes strayed to the plain brown paper bag from the pharmacy, which was still sitting on the coffee table in front of them. She swallowed, suddenly feeling uncertain.

"Don't worry," Robert soothed her, obviously misreading her silence. "This won't hurt."

Miranda glanced at him and felt a curious twist in her chest at his earnest expression. He leaned closer, and the light streaming in through her now-clean windows glinted off his face, making the tips of his long lashes appear red. His eyelids were half-closed in concentration, giving him a slumberous look that sent a trickle of longing down her spine.

She was so intent on watching him that she forgot to keep an eye on the tweezers. They closed over the splinter and yanked. Unfortunately, they also snagged a piece of skin.

"Ouch!" she yelped and jerked her hand away. It hit the sack and knocked it over, spilling its contents onto the floor at his feet.

Miranda closed her eyes. This couldn't be happening to her, she thought in dismay. Of all the gauche, klutzy... She could feel her face burn with embarrassment.

"What are these?" Robert reached for one of the packages.

"If you have to ask, I have a much bigger problem than I thought," she muttered.

Robert looked into her flushed face and felt a surge of protective tenderness. Poor Miranda. She had absolutely no idea of how to go about having an affair. Or else she was a marvelous actress.

He brushed a tumbled curl off her forehead. "Darling Miranda." The soothing timbre of his voice was edged with something different now. Something elementally male that reached out to her emotions on a level she didn't understand, but found unbearably exciting.

Miranda held her breath as his face came closer. Close enough for her to see the tiny laugh lines at the corners of his eyes.

"I wasn't trying to make any demands on you," she said, wanting him to understand, but having trouble thinking coherently.

"Feel free." His breath fanned her cheek, bringing with it the faint flavor of coffee. "It only seems fair, because I intend to make a few demands of my own." His mouth claimed hers with a passion barely held in check.

She grasped his forearms, feeling the muscles bunch beneath her fingertips. Tilting her head, she focused on the pressure his mouth was exerting.

His hand moved to cup the back of her head, and his tongue began to learn her mouth with a boldness that was different from his earlier kisses. This time it was obvious he was making no effort to control his passion. This kiss wasn't an end in itself, but the prelude to much more. The realization exhilarated her and her mouth trembled beneath his. Robert raised his head slightly, nibbling lightly on her lower lip. His teeth grazed the soft skin.

He leaned forward unexpectedly, pushing her off balance, so that she fell backward onto the couch. Her momentary disorientation was immediately superseded by a sense of security when he followed her down and his body loomed protectively over her.

His lips possessively reclaimed hers and his tongue flicked over her teeth.

Miranda coiled her arms around his neck and pulled, wanting to feel more than just his lips. She wanted to feel the weight of his body. Her hands moved fretfully over his back to his waist; tugging his shirt free, they slipped beneath it. The feel of his bare skin against her palms was unbearably erotic. She pushed her hands upward over his hair-roughened chest, shivering at the sensation her action produced. Yet she could feel her body growing hotter, and deep within her there was an aching, something restless.

Impatient now, she tried to tug off his sweater. She wanted to feel his bare skin against her own. Now. A sense of urgency filled her. She had no thought for anything but filling the aching void deep within her.

"Patience, my lovely." Robert yanked his sweater over his head and tossed it behind him.

"No. Now." Miranda splayed her hands against his broad chest. She flexed her fingers, gently digging her nails into his skin. Then she rubbed her hands up and down from his shoulders to his waist, where her progress was impeded by his jeans. His body hair scraped her palms, rasping her flesh. Her need for him twisted a little tighter.

"Robert, you feel so . . ." she said faintly.

"You feel incredible." His hands trembled slightly as he unbuttoned her blouse and slowly separated it as if unwrapping a gift of infinite value.

A small, secretive smile curved her lips; he was nowhere near in control of his own emotions. He was every bit as affected by her as she was by him.

"So very beautiful." Robert trailed his fingers along the lacy edge of her bra. "So soft," he crooned, dropping kisses where his fingers had been.

Miranda tensed at the first touch of his lips against her sensitive flesh and felt her body instinctively arch upward.

Robert took advantage of her movement to slip his hands beneath her and unfasten her bra. It slipped off and onto the floor.

Miranda looked up at him and felt a fierce, elemental pride in her womanhood at the sight of the glow in his eyes.

His hands reverently cupped her breasts, and he lowered his head with a tantalizing slowness. His tongue licked over the tip of her right breast, convulsing the nipple into a tight bud. Miranda gasped and grasped his head, pulling him closer. His mouth closed hotly around the nipple, sucking strongly on it; a jolt of sensation shot through her, pooling in her abdomen. Her skin seemed to tighten as his fingers groped for the snap on her jeans. It finally yielded to his fumbling, and a second later the zipper pulled free.

Robert stood up and, grasping her waistband, yanked off both her jeans and panties, leaving her body bare before his greedy gaze.

Her breathing grew constricted when he kicked off his own jeans.

He looked so . . . so primitively masculine that for a brief second Miranda was afraid of what she had initiated. Then Robert slipped onto the couch beside her. His lips reclaimed hers, hungrily devouring them, and all her doubts evaporated like a mist in the morning sun. This had to be right. There was a sense of inevitability about it. As if she'd been waiting all her life for just this moment.

As if he'd reached the same conclusion, Robert blindly groped for one of the packets on the floor and managed to open it. Then he slipped between her legs and carefully positioned himself. Miranda tensed, unable entirely to suppress her uncertainty.

"Not to worry, my precious," he crooned. "Just relax." He trailed his fingers over her cheek, and she swallowed at the tantalizing touch.

She looked into his eyes, eyes that still seemed to burn with fires she'd ignited, fires only she could quench. Encouraged, she pushed her breasts tightly against his chest, whimpering in pleasure when her action sent a shower of tiny pinpricks of excitement through her.

"I want you to make love to me."

"Yes," he muttered, his eyes glazed as if focused on some inner vision. His mouth came down again, and at the same time he drove deeply into her.

Miranda felt her body struggle to adjust. Infinitesimal tremors began to flow from the point of their fusion, helping her to accept him. Suddenly, without warning, the feeling changed, becoming more urgent. She dug her fingers into his bare hips, trying to pull him closer, wanting to intensify the experience.

"Slowly, Miranda . . . I can't hold back if you . . ." He groaned when she wrapped her legs around his waist.

"Then don't," she urged.

He grasped her shoulders and pushed forward with his lower body. The result was electrifying.

"Robert!" Miranda heard the high, keening sound of her voice. A sudden explosion shook her body, her fingers clutched his biceps, and she began to shake uncontrollably.

The very force of her reaction must have shattered Robert's tenuous grip on his control; he stiffened, then collapsed in a boneless heap on top of her.

Miranda smiled dreamily. She didn't think she ever wanted to move. She sighed happily and snuggled closer. She would be perfectly content to stay here like this for the rest of her natural life.

Unfortunately, the choice was not hers to make. An hour later, she found herself resisting the impulse to beg Robert not to go. To stay and make love to her again. And again. Instead, she firmly reminded herself that modern women didn't cling and firmly closed the door behind him, then stood silent, listening to the retreating roar of the truck's engine as it carried him away.

Miranda poured herself another cup of coffee and wandered to the couch to think about what had happened. Suddenly she noticed that the wall beside the huge china cabinet in front of her seemed to bulge outward ever so slightly. She set down her coffee cup and walked over to it. Curious, she ran her hand over the dingy beige wall. It wasn't just a trick of the light. It really did bulge. Why?

She studied the spot. It was bigger than she'd first thought, extending behind the cabinet. Big enough to provide a hiding place for the pictures? She felt a sudden surge of excitement at the idea. That would explain why she hadn't been able to find them. And it would be a perfect hiding place. No one would ever accidentally stumble across anything hidden in the wall. The more she considered the idea, the more excited she became. The paintings had to be there.

Hurriedly she pushed and shoved the cabinet out of the way. A quick trip to the basement provided her with some tools and she set to work, swinging a crowbar.

Nearly two hours later she was finally ready to admit defeat. She'd uncovered an area six feet long and three feet high, but the only things she'd found besides evidence that the mice were living in the walls, were the pipes leading to the bathroom.

Miranda dropped her crowbar onto the pile of plaster at her feet and waved a hand to clear away the dust. She felt like screaming in frustration. Her brilliant idea had turned out to be a complete bust. In more ways than one. She grimaced as she studied the mess. Everything was covered with plaster dust.

The plaster patch obviously had been the result of plumbing repairs done sometime in the past. She sighed. At least she had something to fill her evening. Cleaning up this mess would take hours. And hours. She shook her head in disgust, then sneezed as her action dislodged a fine cloud of white dust from her hair. Cleaning herself up would take even longer.

And if Robert were here, the cleaning process could take forever. Her breathing grew short at the thought of sharing that small tub with him. Their naked, soap-slicked bodies intertwined. This whole thing would be so much easier if the two of them were searching together. More fun, too. She took a deep breath. If only Robert weren't so closely tied to Axel and the German government.

Maybe she could sound him out about how he felt about returning the paintings anonymously. Could she convince him to forgo the publicity in exchange for them? Would what they had shared outweigh his cousin's claim on his loyalty? She didn't know. She could only hope.

7

MIRANDA SQUINTED at the digital clock on the desk, trying to read the red numbers in the brilliant morning sunshine that was pouring in through her sparkling clean living-room windows. 11:02. She leaned her head back and stared at the dingy ceiling. The day seemed to stretch endlessly in front of her. How was she going to fill the eleven hours or so before she could go to bed? To make matters worse, she didn't just want to fill them with activity, but with a person. Robert Deverill. What she really wanted to do was to spend the whole day making love to Robert, she admitted in a burst of candor that made her feel reckless. Yesterday had been the most fantastic experience of her life. She felt as if she'd finally discovered what all the fuss was about.

Robert had effortlessly shattered all her preconceived ideas about sex and its importance in the general scheme of things. It didn't matter one whit that she couldn't trust him. Nor did it matter that she didn't have the vaguest idea where their relationship was headed.

She could deal with any complications that might arise, she assured herself. Today she felt as if she could deal with anything. She was a desirable woman and relished the feeling.

But much though she wanted to go to the lodge, she resisted the temptation. Robert was used to sophisticated women, and sophisticated women didn't go chasing after their lovers. She'd let him make the next move. And judging by how long it took him to do so would give her some idea of how much he valued what they'd shared. In the meantime she needed something to pass the time.

Something besides finding the missing paintings. Her eyes automatically skittered to the gaping hole in the wall. She grimaced in frustration. Where could Henry have hidden the blasted things? Not in the basement. She'd searched every nook and cranny down there. The floor was unbroken concrete, the walls were of stone, and the mortar between them was of a uniform color. Henry couldn't have removed any of the stones and then secreted the paintings behind them. The basement's ceiling was simply the bare underside of the upstairs floorboards. Nothing but a spider could be hidden there. The basement was out. Which left the attic and the first floor. And she'd already searched in, under and around every piece of furniture, box and trunk in both places.

She remembered her doubts about the flooring in the attic. Could Henry have pried up a few boards, shoved the paintings between the floor joists and then renailed the flooring? It was certainly possible, but in order to find out, she was going to have to rip up a good deal of the attic floor.

She cringed at the thought. Old and decrepit as this house was, any assault on the floors might well have horrendous repercussions.

A muttered clank from the register caught her attention and with a sigh of resignation she got up to put more wood into the ancient furnace. When she emerged from the basement, she peered out the living-room window to check the sky for snow clouds. A flash of movement in the stand of pine trees that lined the back road to the lodge caught her eye. She pressed her nose against the icy window in an attempt to see who it was, tilting her head to one side to shut out the glare from the sparkling-white snow.

Her heartbeat stopped for a second, then sped up as Robert's truck emerged from the trees. Exhilaration gripped her. What they'd shared yesterday had to have meant something to him or he'd never have come back so soon. Hastily she jumped back, not wanting him to think she was spending her time mooning about, waiting for him to show up.

How did one greet a lover the day after? she wondered uncertainly. If she followed her own inclinations, she'd fling her arms around him and kiss him senseless. But that didn't seem like a very sophisticated response, and whatever else Robert might or might not be, he was definitely sophisticated.

The knock on the door froze her thought processes. *Play it cool,* she urged herself. Hoping that the intense excitement she was feeling wasn't visible, she opened the door, then gasped as a blast of frigid air slammed into her at twenty miles an hour. Her skin felt as if it had just been pierced by thousands of tiny needles.

Hastily she moved aside to let him in, then pushed the door shut behind him. "How cold is it out there, anyway?" She latched onto the weather as a safe subject.

"About fifteen. But it's the wind chill that gets to you."

"Wrong. Everything about this weather gets to me."

Robert studied Miranda for a brief, frustrated moment. All morning he'd been counting the minutes until he could escape the seemingly incessant demands of running the lodge and get over here to see her. And now that he was actually here, she was treating him with a casualness he found daunting.

Why didn't she kiss him? Hadn't she felt what he'd felt yesterday? Could she really be using him? Could he have entirely misread the situation as well as her character? Suddenly he remembered her embarrassment when her sack of condoms had spilled. Perhaps she was merely shy? According to Axel's report, she had led a very conventional life to date. Married while still too young to have known what she wanted out of life and now newly divorced.

Maybe his best bet was to play it casually, too, so as not to scare her off. At least not before he'd had a chance to fully explore their physical reaction to each other. Miranda might or might not have had enough experience to appreciate just how unique it had been, but he certainly had.

"Actually, you're a lot like the weather," he said, trying to sound offhand.

"You mean cold?" She frowned and he wondered what she was feeling.

"No. Everything about you gets to me." The sudden flare that lit her dark eyes encouraged him to continue. He put his arms around her and, when she snuggled closer, tightened his hold possessively.

He nuzzled the tiny blue vein on her temple, breathing in her fragrant, flowery scent. Her hair was like silk against his face and her skin like satin beneath his gently questing lips as they wandered over her cheek.

Miranda twisted restlessly in his grasp, wanting the pleasure of his lips upon her own. Wanting to feel their pressure. Their taste. She wriggled slightly, freeing her arms, then reached to grasp his head. Her mouth met his in a sizzling sensation of sparks. Incoherently murmuring her satisfaction, she shivered as the sensation permeated her, creating a trembling deep within.

The kiss wasn't enough, she admitted. She wanted to make love to him again, wanted to feel his body pressed against hers without the inhibiting factor of clothes. But how was she supposed to get him from the stage of "Hello, I'm glad you stopped by this morning," to "Let's jump into bed and make love"? According to what she'd always heard from her unmarried girlfriends, men didn't have anything on their minds but sex. But Robert seemed to be the exception to the rule. In fact—she swallowed a rueful smile—that description seemed to fit her more closely than him.

Robert let go of Miranda as he became aware of the hole in the wall. He hunched and peered into the dusty opening, then looked over his shoulder and caught the guilty expression that flitted across Miranda's face. A sense of excitement gripped him. She must have had reason to think that the—whatever—was hidden in the walls. What she needed was a metal detector. It would register anything of metal, and art objects would undoubtedly have some kind of metal in them, such as gold.

"Plumbing problems?" he asked.

"No," she responded automatically, then could have bitten her tongue in frustration. Agreeing would have explained the hole very nicely.

"Let me guess." He got to his feet. "You've decided to chase the mice into the walls?"

Miranda eyed him in frustration, beginning to sympathize with some of his excuses. This spur-of-the-moment lying wasn't easy. Maybe this was the time to try to enlist his help in locating the paintings? She studied his firm jawline. Then again, maybe it wasn't. Doubts began to creep in. Maybe she should wait awhile. Bringing the theft into the open might spell the end of their relationship, and she wanted to avoid that, even more than she wanted to find the paintings.

"Yes?" He took revenge for her query in the bedroom closet.

She had an inspiration. "I tripped."

"Tripped?"

"Yes. And I fell into the wall," she claimed, hoping he wouldn't remember that the china cabinet had been there.

"You're telling me your body did all that damage?"

"Actually I was carrying something," she elaborated, then hurriedly changed the subject. "What brings you over so early?"

"A couple of things," he improvised. "You remember those desserts of yours from yesterday?"

"No, the *recipes* were mine. I disclaim all responsibility for what your cook did to them."

"Since they are your recipes, how would you like a part-time job, baking desserts?" he said, trying to make it sound like a spur-of-the-moment suggestion, when in fact, he'd spent most of the morning trying to come up with an idea that would bring her to the lodge. It had seemed flawless. Not only would it insure that he could count on seeing her for at least part of each day, but would also allow him access to her house to locate the stolen art before she could find it. He felt his skin chill at the thought of what might happen to her if she did indeed try to fence the art on the black market. Which she might well be planning on doing. He faced the fact squarely. It was clear that she wanted to buy out her ex-husband, and that was going to take money. Lots of money; which brought him full circle.

"No, thanks," she said, having no doubt about his motives. He wanted easy access to her house while she was busy elsewhere.

He backed off quickly at her prompt refusal. "Actually, I have an alternate idea."

"Yes?" Miranda's spirits soared, then plummeted when he continued.

"It's about buying your farm. You could sell me all but a couple of acres up by the county road. I'd even arrange to have this house moved there for you. Then you'd still have the original house and some of the land and I'd have my resort."

"I'd also have my ancestors turning in their graves." She refused automatically, even though she found this latest idea rather intriguing. But she could hardly agree until she found those blasted paintings.

"Would you care to try for a third idea?" she asked.

"How about coming into town with me?" he asked.

"I'd love to." She jumped at the chance to spend time with him. "Are you going into town for any specific purpose?"

"Today's the Methodist church's Christmas bazaar, so I want to pick up a few decorations for the lodge and see if any of the handicrafts being sold might be suitable for the gift shop."

"I have a couple of things to do in town while you do that," Miranda said; this would be an excellent opportunity to see the lawyer who'd handled her uncle's estate and try to find out if he knew anything about the paintings. Maybe Henry had some things in storage somewhere. Perhaps he'd made a bequest to someone else.

He hadn't. Miranda suppressed a sigh of frustration as she finished reading his will. It was simple and straightforward. Henry had left his investments in trust for her three half brothers and all the rest of his property, real and imagined, to her. She hadn't even needed the politely hovering lawyer to explain it to her. It was crystal clear and provided not one clue as to what he'd done with the stolen paintings.

If Henry's lawyer had thought her desire to read the will strange, he'd kept his thoughts to himself. And, when she'd handed the will back to him, he'd walked her to the door of his office and waved to her as she set off down the street.

Miranda bent her head against the brisk wind and hurried down the town's main street, intent on reaching the Methodist church and Robert as quickly as possible.

She ran into him as she rounded the corner, cannoning into what seemed like an immovable force. Robert reached out and grasped her arm to hold her steady. A melting sensation shot through her, a sensation that was in no way diminished by the layers of material separating their bodies. Startled, Miranda looked into his narrowed eyes.

The gleam in them made her feel shy and she lowered her eyes, to find herself staring at the box he was holding under his arm. Acme's Best Metal Detector, she read from the printing on the side. A metal detector? She read the words again to be sure.

"What are you going to use that for?" she asked as she fell into step.

"What?" He silently cursed the garrulous clerk who had delayed him at the hardware store. He'd planned to have the metal detector hidden in the back of his pickup before he met her.

"That metal detector." She gestured toward the box. "What are you going to do with it up here in the dead of winter?"

"We had a customer who dropped his car keys in the snow last week and it took us hours to find them. With a metal detector finding car keys will be a snap," he lied.

To his relief, she didn't seem to find anything unusual in his response.

"Did you find out what you needed to know from Henry's lawyer?" Robert tossed the detector into the back of the truck.

"Uh-huh," she muttered as she climbed into the cab. Even though the interior of the truck wasn't much warmer than the street, simply being out of the wind was a relief. Miranda watched Robert round the truck's hood. Not even his bulky parka could hide the graceful movement of his superbly conditioned body. She wished she could have seen him play tennis. He must have been a joy to watch, running around the court in shorts, with a thin, sweat-soaked shirt plastered to his chest. A surge of desire twisted through her stomach and raced to her nerve endings.

Robert eyed her flushed features and started the engine. "Your face is all red from the force of the wind," he observed.

No, she thought ruefully. Not from the force of the wind. She watched Robert out of the corner of her eye as he steered the truck over the ice-slicked road. He was capable of filling any number of gaps in her emotional life. But what about afterward, when he lost interest and moved on? As he surely would. She hadn't been able to hold Jim's interest, and he was, in truth, a rather mediocre specimen of manhood. Robert Deverill, on the other hand, was not only physically gorgeous but also wealthy, sophisticated and famous. He could have as many affairs with as many beautiful, equally sophisticated women as he cared to work into his schedule. The unpalatable fact irritated her, and she scowled. She didn't like to think of him kissing other women as he'd kissed her. Or any other way, for that matter.

"My driving isn't that bad." Robert's rueful voice broke into her disquieting thoughts.

"Sorry, I was just thinking."

"About selling the farm to me?" He gave her a hopeful look.

"No. And if you don't keep your eyes on the road, your driving will go directly from not bad to catastrophic. Actually," she added slowly, "I'm kind of surprised you haven't sold out yourself. I mean, as a tennis player you must have been used to warm climates, big cities, lots of interesting people around and things going on," she probed, all at once intensely curious about him.

"You don't know much about the upper echelons of tennis, do you."

"I read the papers like everyone else," she said defensively.

"Which ones? The ones that run headlines about space aliens impregnating octogenarians?"

"All I meant was that sports figures lead fishbowl lives."

"I'm not a sports figure. I'm me, Robert Deverill. And I'll tell you something else. It doesn't matter how much natural talent you're born with. If you don't spend years of hard work developing that talent, you'll never make it to the top, let alone stay there."

"It doesn't sound like a very interesting life," she said candidly. "In fact, it sounds like a real drag."

"In some ways it was," Robert conceded. "I traveled all over the world, and yet I rarely had time to do more than make a hurried trip to the nearest tourist attraction. And one motel room is pretty much like any other motel room, no matter where in the world it's located.

"But it wasn't all bad. I really loved tennis. Especially in the beginning. And the money was great," he added honestly.

"But why buy a ski lodge?" she persisted. "Why not a summer resort that features tennis?"

"It's a strange thing . . ." he said slowly, "but if you're very good at something, a lot of people think that you should be able to teach them to be as good. It took me exactly two weeks to realize that I might be a great tennis player, but I was a lousy tennis teacher. I have no patience whatsoever with adults who won't listen to what I'm trying to tell them."

"Welcome to the real world."

Robert slowed the truck to a crawl as he approached the turnoff to her farm. Even so, the heavy truck skidded slightly. "I think you'd better come through the lodge road when you go out," he said. "It'll add a little distance to your trip to town, but I keep that road well plowed and sanded. If my truck is having problems holding the road, then that windup toy of yours wouldn't stand a chance. Why you bought that thing—"

"I didn't buy it. I leased it," she retorted. "I wanted to see if I liked the model before I committed myself to it."

"Repeat after me, 'I don't like that model,'" Robert said emphatically.

"You don't like the model," she said with an innocent grin. "You didn't have to tell me that. I'm great at reading slurs, especially when they're stated repeatedly. Just because you favor bulky trucks . . ."

"I favor appropriateness. In the winter I drive this truck. In the summer I drive a Porsche."

"Porsche!" Miranda blinked in surprise. "You've got a Porsche? Where is it?"

"In the garage on blocks. I'm not going to risk it on these mountain roads in winter."

"I always wanted a Porsche," she said dreamily. "A gold Porsche. If it were mine, I'd take it out on the highway and let the wind rush through my hair as I go a hundred and fifty down the road."

"There isn't a road this side of Nevada where it's safe to do that kind of speed," he pointed out. He slowed to a crawl as they approached the farmhouse.

"Will you let me drive your Porsche?" she asked eagerly.

"No."

Miranda heaved a regretful sigh at his answer, but wasn't really surprised.

"Are you going to sulk?" he asked curiously.

"Please, allow me a moment of respectful silence to bury my shattered aspirations."

"Are you mad at me?" He pulled up in front of her porch and cut the engine.

"No," she replied with perfect honesty. "If I had a Porsche, I wouldn't let anyone else drive it, either."

"It's not that I won't let anyone else drive it. It's just that you..." He paused; there was no tactful way to say that she sounded like a maniac behind the wheel.

Miranda eyed him closely. "You're wise to shut up."

He cupped his hand around her chin and tilted her head. Miranda could feel the calluses on his palm, and the sensation excited her unbearably.

"Allow me to make it up to you," he murmured.

The click of his seat belt sounded like the crack of a rifle shot in the deep silence. Miranda closed her eyes and gave free rein to her excitement.

She ran the tip of her tongue over her bottom lip, then peeked at him through her lashes to see how he responded to her deliberate provocation. A fresh kick of excitement shortened her breathing at the gleam in his hazel eyes.

Robert followed the path of her tongue with his thumb and a salty taste filled her mouth. When he didn't follow his caress with a kiss, she decided to take the initiative. "I want to kiss you," she whispered.

"Believe me, the feeling is mutual," he said, but still made no move toward her.

Intrigued, Miranda moved closer. "You know, you have the most determined jaw." She ran her fingers across his chin, feeling a new ferment when he shuddered.

"Thank you, I think," he muttered.

"And it feels so interesting. Kind of like rasped silk." She pressed a kiss exactly upon the middle of his chin. "And not only that, but you—"

"Talk too much." Robert scooped her up and pulled her across his lap. His mouth met hers with a rough, masculine hunger that she found intoxicating. With a sigh she surrendered to the sensation, willingly parting her lips to allow the invasion of his questing tongue. It ran lightly over her teeth, causing a shimmer of sensation; she opened her mouth still wider. His tongue engaged hers in a sensual duel that had no losers, only winners. For a moment, time and place ceased to have any meaning. All that mattered was sensation.

Finally Robert raised his head and looked into her slumberous eyes. "There," he whispered softly. "Isn't that better than playing Russian roulette with my Porsche?"

Miranda stared blankly at him. His words echoed through her mind. She had the sinking feeling that continuing to kiss him could eventually prove more dangerous than driving a high-powered sports car ever would.

Groping for something, anything to return a sense of normalcy to her world, she finally blurted, "I'm hungry."

Robert laughed. "I couldn't have put it better myself."

"Uh, yes, well . . ." She flushed. "Be that as it may, I have lots to do and I'd better get into the house."

"You could come back to the lodge and have lunch with me," he coaxed.

"I'd better not." She forced herself to refuse. She'd already wasted the morning. She couldn't afford to fritter away the afternoon, too. There were all those boards in the attic to rip up. Not only that, but she was a modern woman of the nineties, she reminded herself. A sophisticated woman didn't allow her lover to become the center of her life, and if she wasn't careful, that was exactly where Robert would end up.

"Maybe tomorrow," she said firmly. "Right now I have a lot to do." Opening the cab door, she climbed out, disappointed that he made no attempt to get her to change her mind.

8

OH, GREAT! Exactly what she needed to add a little more spice to her life. No heat. Miranda eyed the scattering of logs lying on the floor of the woodshed. She'd meant to see about ordering more firewood when she'd gone into town yesterday, but somehow, in the excitement of being with Robert, the need had slipped her mind.

It most definitely was a need. Miranda shivered as the wind buffeted the small, rickety shed. She glanced down at her watch. Three-thirty. Even if she ordered firewood right now, she probably couldn't get it delivered today. On the other hand, if she didn't order it now, she might not even get it tomorrow. She headed back to the house.

The telephone directory's Yellow Pages provided the information she wanted, but as she'd feared, the earliest she was able to get a promise of delivery was for the following morning.

Miranda hung up and considered the situation. She would run out of wood to feed the furnace sometime late this evening. She shivered again. Shortly thereafter it would get cold. Very cold. Much too cold to stay here overnight. She could go into town to a motel, but that would leave the house unprotected if Robert should happen to come by. For a brief second, her thoughts strayed to Robert and his well-heated lodge. Her heartbeat accelerated; she also remembered the warmth of his kisses.

No. She firmly squelched the impulse to go to him. Showing up on his doorstep, with what was bound to sound like the flimsiest of excuses, would look as if she were trying to take advantage of the fact that they had made love. As if she were trying to force the pace of their relationship.

Miranda pressed her lips together in determination. She'd stay here and turn into an icicle before she'd do that. She hadn't begun to sort out the nuances of their affair, but one thing she did know, at present they were equals. Both freely giving and taking, and she had no intention of doing anything that might upset that delicate balance.

She was staring out the window when suddenly a cardinal flew across her line of vision. She blinked and watched the beautiful bird flit from tree to tree. Trees! There were trees all around the farmhouse. Trees were nothing more than firewood in the making. Not only that, but she vaguely remembered seeing a good-sized saw hanging on the wall in the barn—a saw she could use to cut down one of those trees.

That was the ticket, she thought happily. All she had to do was chop up a tree and burn it. Buoyed by her inspiration, she slipped into her coat and hurried to the barn.

Miranda had a few qualms when she took a good look at the saw. Six feet long, with handles at both ends, it was probably meant for two people to use. But that didn't mean that one couldn't use it, she assured herself. It would just take twice as long.

Miranda picked up one end of the saw and, dragging it behind her, left the barn in search of a sacrificial victim. She rejected several trees that looked big enough to break a bone if they accidentally fell on her and finally settled on a small maple with a trunk about eight inches in diameter.

Since there was no one to hold the other end of the saw in the air, she had to dig away the foot of loose snow at the base of the tree in order to rest it on the ground. Unfortunately, with the saw on the ground, she had to get down on her knees in order to pull it back and forth. A few tentative shoves were sufficient to convince her that sawing down a tree was not going to be an easy task. She sighed. Maybe spending the night huddled under a blanket wasn't such a bad idea, after all. Pioneer women must have had constitutions of iron to put up with conditions like these. To say nothing of iron muscles. She dragged the saw toward her with grim determination and tried to shove it forward.

It didn't budge. Determined, Miranda pushed all the harder. To her shocked surprise, the blade buckled and sprang back, catching her arm about two inches above the wrist. It neatly sliced through both parka and skin.

She stared at the bright red blood gushing through the tear in her brand-new coat. She'd seen far too many kitchen accidents not to know the significance of the way the blood was spurting. That blasted blade had managed to cut an artery.

With more speed than finesse, she ripped off her scarf and wrapped it around her injured arm right above the wound. Using a small branch lying at her feet, she tightened the makeshift tourniquet. To her relief, the flow slowed to a trickle.

"So far, so good," she encouraged herself, averting her eyes from the red stain that now marred the pristine whiteness of the snow. Blindly she looked around, trying to think, but the sound of blood drumming in her ears was interfering with her thought processes.

Robert. His name welled out of her subconscious like an answer to a prayer. If she could just get to Robert, he'd know what to do. She turned and staggered toward the car. It took her three tries to start the car and the half-mile trip to the lodge seemed interminable.

Miranda pulled up in front of the lodge. Not even bothering to try to park, she cut the engine and stumbled out. She felt nauseous and light-headed and what was worse, could no longer feel her injured arm.

She started across the lobby on unsteady legs, intending to ask Maud where Robert could be found, but it proved unnecessary. A young woman standing nearby took one look at the blood dripping off Miranda's fingers and launched into a series of piercing screams that would have done a Valkyrie proud. To Miranda's infinite relief, Robert seemed to materialize in front of her.

"What happened?" His calm voice immediately dispelled the feeling of unreality fogging her mind.

"I'm dripping blood all over your freshly polished floor," she mumbled. "Aren't you glad you don't have carpeting in your lobby?" For some reason the idea struck her as hilarious and she began to giggle.

Robert turned and spoke to someone outside her line of vision. "Call the hospital and tell them that Miranda's cut her wrist and we'll be there as soon as we can." He hurriedly slipped into the leather jacket Maud tossed to him.

"As soon as we can," Miranda parroted, feeling a blessed sense of relief wash over her. She'd been right. Robert did know what to do.

Miranda gasped when he swept her up and into his arms, intensifying her disorientation. She leaned her whirling head against his shoulder. It felt solid, hard. Safe. Infinitely safe, as nothing in her life had ever felt before.

"Here, let me help." A guest ran to open the door and Robert carried her through.

"Thank you." Miranda gave the man a wobbly smile. Now that she was safe in Robert's arms, the compulsion to stay alert was fading.

Robert hurriedly placed Miranda in his pickup, adjusted the tourniquet and sprinted to the driver's side. Jumping in, he slammed the door shut.

Miranda gasped again when he put the truck into gear and sped down the driveway to the accompaniment of shrieking tires.

"What happened?" he repeated, swinging the truck onto the highway on two wheels and a prayer.

"I had an accident with the saw."

"Saw?" He shot her a quick glance. If she'd taken to cutting into the walls in her search for the stolen art, she'd be lucky if the house didn't tumble down around her ears.

To her relief, Robert didn't ask any more embarrassing questions. Instead, he concentrated on driving on the snowy roads. As he approached the hospital, he accelerated the truck past the sign pointing to the emergency room entrance, and came to a bone-jarring halt under a portico, in front of a pair of sliding glass doors. Cutting the engine, he sprinted around the cab and flung open the passenger door.

"I can walk!" Miranda protested when he swept her into his arms once more.

He ignored her and carried her through the doors.

"Mr. Deverill?" A nurse was waiting just inside. At Robert's nod, she continued. "Just put her in this wheelchair and we'll take her back to Emergency."

Robert gently set Miranda down. "I'll go with her."

"You will move your truck. It's blocking the entrance," the nurse stated.

"All right, I'll move the truck," Robert reluctantly agreed. He lightly touched Miranda's white cheek with his forefinger. "Be brave and, if you need me, just scream."

"I will." She gave him a weak smile, then the nurse pushed the chair down a brightly lit corridor toward a pair of doors marked No Admittance to Unauthorized Personnel.

"That's quite some man you got there," the nurse said.

"Yes, indeed he is." A soft, dreamy sigh escaped Miranda's lips.

"Don't you dare pass out on me until I get your particulars," the nurse ordered.

"Particulars?" Miranda tried to raise her head. It proved a mistake. She felt herself slipping down into a multicolored, whirling vortex.

It was almost an hour, an hour Miranda barely remembered later, before she was on her way home again with a neat, white bandage covering her wrist. She leaned her head against the seat and closed her eyes, almost immediately slipping into a deep sleep.

She awoke to a sensation of movement. As if she were sailing on a relatively calm sea. She breathed deeply, frowning in confusion when she smelled leather instead of salt water.

Leather? She forced open heavy eyelids and found her field of vision limited to brown leather. Robert's brown leather jacket. She felt awful. Her head ached, her arm ached, and her stomach was doing sit-ups. All she wanted to do was to crawl into a hole and hibernate till spring.

"Stop that infernal racket!" she heard Mrs. Kolcheck yell. "You're—" Miranda heard her gasp, then saw her hastily step out of the way.

"Is she all right?" Mrs. Kolcheck demanded, trailing along behind them. Robert crossed the kitchen and headed toward a part of the inn that Miranda had never been in before.

"Dave said her whole hand was just hanging by a thread of skin," Mrs. Kolcheck went on, speaking with a ghoulish relish that made Miranda's stomach twist.

"Dave should have used his eyes instead of his imagination," Robert said; Miranda merely groaned. "All she did was nick an artery."

Miranda saw Mrs. Kolcheck squeeze around Robert to open a door, then press herself against the corridor wall.

"How about a cup of hot tea?" she suggested.

"Bring a whole pot and something cold," Robert called over his shoulder. "She's supposed to drink lots of liquids."

"I'll see to it." Mrs. Kolcheck bustled away, clearly pleased to have something to do.

Robert carried Miranda into a bedroom and gently set her down upon the huge bed that dominated the room.

"Where am I?" she asked feebly.

"This is my suite," Robert said, sitting down on the bed.

Miranda blinked at him. She felt light-headed to the point of faintness. "Suite?" She struggled to understand the word.

"I live in a suite on the ground floor of the inn," he explained patiently. "It lets me get away from my guests. If not the staff," he added ruefully.

"I don't want to inconvenience you. . . ."

"You did that when you refused to sell the farm to me. It's been all downhill from there."

She closed her eyes at his words and promptly fell asleep.

The pain in her arm finally woke her. It radiated from the cut, setting her nerve endings on fire. She shifted restlessly, gasping when her movement put pressure upon the site of her tetanus shot. She peered at it. The area around the shot was red, swollen and extremely painful.

Gingerly she rolled out of bed and stood up, keeping a death grip on the bedpost until her wobbly legs firmed somewhat. Curious, she looked around the room. It was well worth the look. The cherry furniture had a patina that only centuries of loving care could bring. The thick, cream and pale blue Aubusson carpet was a soft cloud beneath her bare feet. She slowly walked to the triple dresser and examined the half-dozen, silver-framed photographs there.

She picked up a picture of a couple who appeared to be in their sixties. The woman had Robert's smile and the man his firm jawline. His parents, she surmised. She set it down and looked at the rest. There was a picture of a very young Robert sitting on a pony. The reins were held by an equally young, blond boy. Axel? There was another picture with Axel in it. This time he was much older and the horse was much bigger. Her skin chilled; the uniform he was wearing reminded her of the stolen paintings.

First thing tomorrow morning she was going to get back to the farmhouse and find those blasted things, she thought in frustration. She didn't dare stay here and give Robert an opportunity to get his hands on them first.

Miranda found the bathroom and splashed cold water on her face; it looked flushed.

She walked back into the bedroom to find Robert sitting on the bed, clearly waiting for her. She let her eyes wander appreciatively over his body. He was wearing a pair of blue pajama bottoms and nothing else. The thin cotton clung to his long legs, clearly delineating his powerful thigh muscles. His broad chest was covered with a liberal coating of dark brown hair.

Her fingers itched to touch him. She wanted to rub her hands over his chest. To explore the muscles beneath. Her eyes continued their upward journey, over his firm chin, lingering fractionally on the line of his lips, noting his disheveled hair. She watched him walk toward her, his bare feet making no sound on the thick carpet.

Robert paused in front of her, narrowing his eyes as he studied her face. He reached out and pressed the back of his hand against her flushed cheek.

"Damn! You're hot."

Only for you, Miranda thought and giggled.

"Are you delirious?"

"If I were delirious, I wouldn't know I was, would I?" she pointed out. "What time is it?"

"A little after midnight."

"Midnight!"

"I don't like this fever. I wonder if your cut's infected?"

"It's because of the tetanus shot. The nurse says almost everyone reacts badly to it. Could I please have a drink of something cold with bubbles? And do you mind if I borrow one of your pajama tops, since you don't seem to use them?"

"If you insist." His voice deepened, and Miranda felt an answering twist of excitement. "They're in the bottom dresser drawer. I'll go see about your drink."

Miranda watched him leave before opening the dresser drawer to find the matching blue top to the bottoms he was wearing. She quickly stripped off her clothes and slipped it on, studying herself in the mirror. Her tousled curls and feverishly glittering eyes gave her a sensual, wanton look that was reinforced by the pajama top's deep V and her long, bare legs visible beneath the hem.

Carefully she climbed between the smooth sheets, stretching her legs into the cool depths. She leaned back against the mound of soft, down pillows and sighed in satisfaction. Her head was relatively clear and her stomach felt fine. Only her arm hurt. She shifted restlessly, trying to find a more comfortable position. She couldn't.

She ran her fingers through her curls, pushing them off her forehead. This was going to be a long night. And where was Robert with her cold drink? she wondered fretfully. Surely it didn't take that long to open a can.

Ten minutes later he returned, carrying two cans of soda.

"What took you so long?" she demanded and was immediately ashamed of the querulous note in her voice. "I'm sorry," she apologized. "I'm feeling a little out of sorts."

"It's only to be expected."

He opened one of the cans and handed it to her.

Miranda's hot fingers closed gratefully around the icy container. Briefly she pressed the can against her forehead, then took a long, satisfying swallow. Feeling fractionally cooler, she smiled at Robert. "Aren't you going to join me?" She nodded toward the other can.

"No, you're drinking both of them."

"I said I wanted a drink, not a deluge," she protested.

"I just called the hospital to ask them about your arm, and they weren't any too happy to hear that you haven't drunk anything yet."

"Life's full of disappointments," she muttered.

"Keep drinking," he urged. "And while you're about it, take these." He handed her two aspirin.

Miranda took them with the last of the first can of soda and set it down upon the bedside table. "Actually, I don't feel all that bad."

She reached out and ran her fingers down his arm. A slight tremor beneath his skin heightened her awareness.

Robert stared assessingly into her eyes. They glittered with a fevered brightness that sent an answering curl of excitement shafting through him. One that he made a valiant, if totally ineffective, effort to stifle.

"Darling Miranda," he said huskily. He framed her cheeks between his hands and lightly kissed the tip of her nose. "You need to rest."

She captured his head between her hands.

"Wrong. I need to be humored," she murmured wickedly, sending a flush of desire over his cheekbones.

Robert leaned forward, then caught himself. What kind of man was he? Miranda was ill. She'd not only cut her arm, but had a fever, and all he could think about was making love to her. He wanted to kiss her senseless, but it was obvious that he was the one who had no sense. He was acting like a rutting bull. Like a man in love.

Shock rippled through him; the unexpected idea ricocheted with the impact of a bullet. He stared into her sparkling eyes and tried to absorb the hows and whys, but no answer was to be found there. All he could see was a reflection of the hunger that was coursing through him. He felt the muscles in his jaw bunched as he tried again to contain his feelings long enough to think.

How could he have fallen in love with her? He'd never meant to give any woman the power to hurt him emotionally. But Miranda could, he admitted uneasily.

How did she feel about him? he wondered. Was it possible she loved him, too? There was no way he could know. She probably didn't know herself. Her divorce was so recent that she could hardly have moved far enough beyond it to be thinking in terms of commitment to anyone else yet. To be sure, she had recovered enough to become physically involved with him. Very involved. Satisfaction filled him.

He found his hand coming up to stroke her satiny-smooth cheek as he tried to plan. He'd allow the relationship to develop at its own pace while she distanced herself from her divorce and he'd explore how he really felt about her. In the meantime... Longingly he focused on her lips, not allowing his eyes to drift lower.

"Robert, dear, dear Robert." Miranda trailed her fingers along his jawline, and the flowery scent of her perfume drifted into his lungs, vividly illustrating the impact of her femininity.

"Miranda, dear, dear Miranda." He captured her hand and kissed the backs of her fingers. "We've got to remember that you aren't feeling up to par."

Her throaty chuckle hovered in the air between them. "You, on the other hand, feel great," she said.

"But..."

"Honestly, Robert," she grumbled, "what do I have to do? Send you an engraved invitation?" She leaned forward on her knees and, putting her hands upon his chest, pushed. Caught off balance, he fell backward onto the bed with her sprawled across his chest.

He swallowed hard, trying to ignore the gaping front of her pajama top, which gave him an unobstructed view to her waist. He shut his eyes in an attempt not to see her perfectly formed breasts, only to become excruciatingly aware of the feel of them. The thin cotton of that garment was no barrier at all.

Miranda seductively wriggled her abdomen against his thighs, causing his manhood to tighten with an almost painful intensity. She laughed with gleeful delight at the instinctive response he was incapable of hiding.

"Miranda," he said desperately, "one of us has to use their head."

"Okay." She buried her face against his neck and began to nuzzle the skin behind his ear. Her tongue darted out to lick the spot, and his muscles jerked at the provocation. "You use your head. I'll use your body." She caught his earlobe between her teeth and lightly bit it. Her breath was hot against his skin and her mouth even hotter as she began to suck on it.

"We can't . . ." He made an almost superhuman effort to ignore the urgings of his body; all he wanted was to flip her onto her back and bury himself deep within her. He reached to push her away with a hand that trembled. Unfortunately for his noble intentions, his hand brushed against the bare flesh of her hip. Miranda sighed with audible pleasure at his touch, and the sound pierced his shaky self-control, irrevocably shattering it.

Miranda began to trace the indentations of his ear with the tip of her tongue and he surrendered. "You win."

"Oh, no," she murmured against his chin. "We both win."

He chuckled. "Be that as it may, just to be on the safe side, you set the pace. I don't want to accidentally hurt you." He shifted slightly, allowing her legs to slip between his. He could feel the long, sleek length of them against his much rougher skin and grew restless.

"Me set the pace?" Miranda raised her head and stared at him, obviously intrigued by the idea.

"Yes," he muttered.

She studied his harshly carved features for a long moment with a mischievous expression. "Can I do anything I like?"

"As long as what you like has speed at the top of the list. I'm not sure how long I can last."

Miranda giggled and a curl tumbled over her forehead, giving her the appearance of a very sexy cherub. "Men have no staying power," she chortled.

She leaned over him and began to string kisses across his face like a butterfly drifting aimlessly from flower to flower. He found the experience torturous. He wanted to crush her against him, wanted to absorb her into his very being, and she was doling out insubstantial kisses.

"Miranda!"

She paused and blinked as if trying to clear her thoughts. "You don't like it?" she finally asked.

"I can't stand it. I want you. The essence of you. Not all this . . ."

"Foreplay," she said in all seriousness. "It's called foreplay, and I like it. In fact, I think I could become addicted."

"I think I could go crazy," he groaned.

"Well, in that case . . ." She sat up, her soft hips pressing against his flat abdomen and her thighs gripping each side of his waist. Slowly, with the precision of an artist intent on getting exactly the right effect, she began to unbutton the pajama top she was wearing.

Robert clenched his fists to keep from ripping the thin material away. His breath caught in his throat as the last button came free and she shrugged out of the garment. Her small breasts were taut and firm and he longed to taste them, but seeing her without her pajama top reminded him just how badly swollen her arm was. He was afraid of inadvertently hurting her.

Miranda arched over his chest and slowly began to rub the tips of her breasts against him.

His breath escaped in a loud, whooshing sound, and the exquisitely pleasurable sensation seemed to send a million tiny jolts of electricity through him, making his heart race.

He clenched his teeth; sweat popped out on his forehead. He couldn't take much more of this.

"Robert?" Miranda's voice was husky with need. "Help me. I not quite sure of the logistics of ..."

"Yes," he muttered. "Yes, my precious one." With hands made clumsy by the urgency of his need, he grasped her hips and, lifting her slightly, positioned her above him. Slowly, ever so slowly, he let her slide downward, locking his muscles as he began to penetrate her.

Two times two is four. Four times four is eight. Eighteen times... Frantically he tried to focus his mind on something other than the feel of her hot flesh sheathing him. Of her inner muscles clenching and unclenching around his throbbing penis.

Miranda wriggled her hips slightly and he was lost. Totally, irrevocably lost. The only thing in the universe that mattered was the feel and the touch of her.

He grasped her waist and pulled her down, fitting her pliant body more tightly against him. Miranda uttered a soft, yearning sound deep in her throat that raised gooseflesh on his arms. As if she, too, had finally reached the limits of endurance, she arched her back and ground her hips tighter against him.

Her head was thrown back and her breasts were taut and full, their tips hard with the force of the emotion she was plainly feeling. Her intense pleasure fed his reaction and he could feel himself losing control.

Sensation upon sensation ripped through him, and his body surged upward with a will of its own. Dimly, as if from a great distance, he could feel her convulsing around him; with one last thrust he exploded in her.

Miranda collapsed upon his chest. Feeling intense satisfaction, he cradled her protectively against him.

Robert could hear the even tenor of her breathing as she drifted off to sleep. He found it much more difficult, tortured by his thoughts. Did he really love her? He certainly wanted to *make* love to her. He also wanted to protect her, something unusual for him, he admitted. Normally he saw women as equals who were perfectly capable of taking care of their own problems. With Miranda he had an urge to try to keep her safe. To shield her from the consequences of her own actions. That could be horrendous if she tried to sell Henry's ill-gotten goods on the black market. Not only would the lowlifes who dealt in stolen goods be a danger to her, but Axel would be after her blood. And Axel was not a man to be taken lightly. Robert's arms tightened around Miranda. If he had to, he could handle Axel. He didn't want to do anything to drive a wedge into their relationship, but Miranda was more important to him, he realized with a sense of shock. In a few short days she had become more important to him than a cousin he'd known all his life.

And to complicate matters, there was so much about her he didn't know. He didn't even know exactly how she felt about him. While it was obvious that she enjoyed making love to him, she didn't fully trust him or she would have told him about the art.

His frustration grew as he tried to decide what to do. If he pushed her about the stolen art, she might retreat from him, physically and mentally. His options were extremely limited. About all he could do was step up his own search. If he could just get to it first, then he could return it to Axel before she knew what had happened.

His mouth lifted in a rueful grin. Ah, well, he'd never really enjoyed matches when his opponent hadn't presented a challenge to his skills. And Miranda was certainly doing that. If he could somehow manage to extricate her from her involvement in this mess, then convince her that she loved him and wanted to stay up here at the lodge with him, he would have won the greatest event of his long career. He felt the old familiar kick of adrenaline and smiled in anticipation.

9

THE FAINT, INCESSANT noise finally woke her. Miranda blinked disorientedly, focusing on a colorful print that wasn't supposed to be there. She closed her eyes to repudiate the picture's existence.

Good Lord, she thought in dismay. She was becoming obsessed with art, even seeing the blasted stuff in her sleep. She rolled over, jarring her swollen arm. The pain brought memory flooding back. She was at the lodge. In Robert's suite. More specifically, in Robert's bed. Her eyes snapped open, scanning the other side of the bed. It was empty. The antique clock on the bedside table revealed it was nine-fifteen. She cocked her head and listened to the muffled sounds of people in the distance. Skiers must like to get an early start, she decided ruefully.

Slowly she got out of bed and, slipping on the pajama top she'd so precipitously discarded the night before, went to find Robert. The suite was empty. Miranda frowned in disappointment. Where could he be? At her house? She stiffened slightly. It was possible, in fact, probable. With her sound asleep in his bed, he'd have a good shot at finding the paintings.

Miranda glanced at his desk to see if he had left her a note. The only paper on the gleaming cherry top was a folded sheet of thick white vellum. She picked it up, stiffening when she saw the boldly scrawled "Axel" at the bottom. Squelching her feeling of guilt at reading someone else's mail, she quickly scanned it and her stomach contracted in sudden panic.

According to the letter, Axel had managed to track Uncle Henry's movements to a museum in Munich, where he had worked for three weeks before being discharged and shipped home. A museum that was missing six priceless paintings. Paintings that Axel felt Henry might well have stolen.

Miranda let out her breath in a long, shaky sigh. His conclusions were right on target. But what was worse was the final paragraph, in which he asked Robert to present their conclusions to a local judge and ask for a search warrant.

Miranda hastily replaced the letter. She had to find those paintings first, because she didn't have the slightest doubt that a team of professionals would find them quickly. Time was now of the essence.

She hurried back to the bedroom and awkwardly began to dress. As long as she remembered not to jar her arm, she felt fine. Even the slight fever she'd had last night was gone. Cured by making love with Robert, she thought fancifully. Her fingers stilled, and for a second she paused to savor the memory. A sudden clatter from the hallway on the other side of the bedroom wall shattered her absorption and she opened his closet, looking for a shirt she could borrow.

She picked out a blue cotton one and slipped into it. It was strange—but good—to be wearing his clothes. What was it about Robert Deverill that made her wish they had a future together. He didn't meet many of her requirements. He wasn't particularly patient and certainly wasn't open and aboveboard in his dealings with her. But that didn't seem to matter. She preferred the flesh and blood Robert, imperfections and all.

Miranda studied her slender figure in the mirror, wishing her relationship with Robert were as clear as her reflection. Unfortunately, the situation was complicated by the fact that she had the two things that he wanted—the farm and the purloined paintings. It was possible that he'd first made love to her in order to convince her to turn over both of them. Although he'd seemed more interested in stealing the paintings than in getting her to give them to him, she thought ruefully. And as for his desire to buy the farm, his recent offers had seemed more perfunctory than insistent. As if he'd had something else on his mind. Like their relationship? She sighed. One thing she was certain of. Whatever his motives for starting the affair had been, he was emotionally involved now. There was no way he could have faked his reaction to her last night. The knowledge eased her uncertainty somewhat and she finished dressing, intent on finding Robert.

As she'd suspected, he had left the lodge almost an hour ago. To stoke up her furnace, Maud told her.

"How thoughtful of him." Miranda saw Maud blink in surprise at her wry tone. More likely stoking up his thievish skills, she thought. With a parting smile for the obviously confused Maud, she hastily bought another coat from the ski shop and hurried to the parking lot. Life would be much simpler if she could just sit back and let Robert find those blasted paintings. But she couldn't. Her loyalty to her mother and stepfather demanded that she find them herself.

Her feelings of frustration intensified when it took her four tries to coax the car's cold engine to life. Making a mental note to check with a garage to make sure that she had the proper level of antifreeze for this arctic climate, Miranda carefully drove around the ski lodge to the access road that led to her farmhouse.

Once she emerged from the thick stand of evergreens, she had a clear view of the house and, more specifically, of Robert's truck. Instead of driving up to the house and letting him know she was there, she decided to park behind the barn. Feeling like an extra in a James Bond movie, she carefully closed the car door, not letting it slam, then peered around the side of the barn. When she didn't see anyone, she crossed the open space to the house. With infinite care she tiptoed across the porch and peeked into the window. He was moving some kind of device up and down the wall.

The metal detector! But why was Robert using it on her living-room walls? She sat down underneath the window and tried to think.

She squinted, trying to shut out the glare of the sun as she mentally sifted the possibilities. They were discouragingly few. In fact, other than the idea that he'd taken leave of his senses, she could only think of one. He was locating the nails in the walls in order to find the studs, and she could think of no earthly reason why he would want to do that. Unless . . . Could there be something metallic in the paintings? But what? Lead paint? The notion was ridiculous. She was missing something, but what?

Straightening, she crept to the door. A cautious twist of the knob showed her that it was unlocked and, taking a deep breath, she opened it and stepped inside.

"Let me guess. You're prospecting for gold?" The shocked expression on Robert's face almost made her laugh.

"What are you doing here?" he demanded.

"I think that's my line."

He set down the metal detector. "I came over to stoke your furnace."

"And stayed to search my walls?" She pulled off her cap and ran her fingers through her squashed curls.

"Actually, I was just testing the metal detector to see if it worked," he improvised. "I noticed that it was still in the truck when I arrived, so after I started the fire in the furnace, I decided to try it out by finding the nails in the walls."

Miranda gave him an approving smile. He was really getting much better at this spur-of-the-moment lying. If she didn't find those paintings soon, by the end of the month, he'd be believable.

"What are you doing out of bed?" Robert demanded.

"Where else would I be at ten o'clock in the morning?"

"This is the morning after you tried to saw off your arm," he reminded her. He brushed one particularly unruly curl off her forehead and traced the bridge of her nose. Her chilled skin felt smooth and eminently touchable. "You're far too pale. You should stay in bed. At least for today."

The sound of his husky voice helped to release her from the strange spell that had fallen over her at his light touch. "Nonsense." She tried for a brisk tone, but it merely came out sounding breathless. "I only cut myself."

"What you only cut was an artery," he said dryly. "Why don't you stay with me until your arm heals?"

"No, thank you," she said, refusing to allow herself to give in. There was too much at stake. Her own independence—and her stepfather's career.

"At least spend the night with me so that you won't have to worry about the furnace."

And so we can make love, she thought longingly. At night she could stay close to him so that he wouldn't have time to slip away to search for anything.

"Thank you." She accepted the compromise. "I'd like that."

"Good." His answering smile left her in no doubt that he shared her idea of how to spend the time. "Now sit down, while I go check out your furnace before I leave."

Miranda sat. She wasn't the least bit tired, but apparently nothing was going to convince Robert that she wasn't at death's door. Unless... She scowled at the doorway he'd disappeared through. Unless his concern was merely an excuse to install her at the lodge so that he could search in peace. She sighed. Those infernal paintings were complicating everything.

Robert emerged from the basement a few minutes later, brushing wood chips off the front of his cream-colored Aran sweater and his well-worn jeans. "Everything's fine down there. Either Dave or I will be back later to check on you." His obdurate expression dared her to argue.

"Fine." She gave in to the seductive feeling that someone cared about her well-being.

"In the meantime, call me if anything should go wrong."

"Everything already has," she said ruefully. "What else could possibly go wrong?"

"Seek and ye shall find," he quoted. "Although, considering your track record, trouble will probably come looking for you."

"That's slander," she protested. "I never had any problems before I came up here."

"About your problem . . ."

"You'll have to be more specific," she said dryly.

"I was referring to the desserts Mrs. Kolcheck ruined."

Miranda arched one eyebrow. "It's not my problem. She's your cook."

"And you owe me."

"I have the nasty feeling that I'm going to be making installment payments on that trip to the hospital forever," Miranda grumbled.

"Not that one. This time you owe me for Virgil Selvent."

"Virgil Selvent? I don't know any Virgil Selvent."

"He's the man who delivered the wood you ordered yesterday. He came into the lodge this morning to ask if we knew where to find you. Since you were still asleep, I paid him. So you owe me." He gave her a smug smile.

Miranda giggled at his expression. "As I live and breathe, if it isn't Sir Jasper with a foreclosure on the mortgage. All you need is a mustache to twirl."

"I had one once."

"You did?" She studied him critically, trying to imagine it. She couldn't.

"Uh-huh. It itched, though, so I shaved it off. Now about Virgil . . ."

"I'll write you a check."

"I don't take checks."

"Oh?" Miranda eyed him with sudden interest.

"I'll settle for you consulting with Mrs. Kolcheck."

Miranda sighed in disappointment. "All right, I'll talk to the woman, but don't blame me if you don't like what you find out."

"That's one of the hazards of consulting," he said seriously. "I did some for various tennis clubs when I first retired. Fortunately, before I went mad I stumbled across this place and bought it."

But why had he been here in the first place? Miranda wondered. Had his interest in the stolen paintings come before or after he'd bought the lodge? And exactly where did Axel fit into things?

Robert leaned over and placed a very unsatisfying kiss upon her forehead. "I'll see you later, and in the meantime try not to do anything stupider than usual."

"That opens some exciting possibilities," she muttered, annoyed by his brotherly manner.

"Rest," he ordered.

"I'll do my best," Miranda said as she walked him to the door.

The minute she heard the sound of his truck, she locked the door and forced herself to concentrate on the problem of the paintings. First she'd make herself a pot of coffee and then tackle the attic flooring. While she waited for the coffee to brew, she located the crowbar she'd used to open up the hole in the wall. All too soon the coffee was made so, out of excuses, she put on her coat and headed for the attic.

Miranda shivered convulsively as she left the warmth of downstairs behind. Where to start? Her gaze swept the attic floor. The paintings could be under any of the boards. But even so, it shouldn't be necessary to pry them all up, she finally decided. Ripping up every third one should still allow her to check beneath them. Even if Henry had removed the paintings from their frames and rolled them up, she would still be able to see them.

Gamely she headed to the back of the attic where the floor space was relatively clear. She inserted the tip of the bar between two boards and, using her hip and un-injured arm, managed to pry the board up. It was a lot harder than she'd expected, but she doggedly kept going. Except for brief forays downstairs to drink coffee and warm her frozen toes and fingers, she worked steadily all morning. Even so, she barely managed to loosen a quarter of the boards.

Finally, when the crowbar slipped and hit her hip for what felt like the hundredth time, Miranda decided she'd had enough. She dropped the crowbar onto a battered steamer trunk and carefully made her way down the steep stairs. She was exhausted, as if she'd been working for days instead of hours.

Once downstairs, she stripped off her coat and gloves, tossed them onto a chair and staggered to the couch. The room's warmth seemed to be sapping what little energy she had left.

She checked the time on the clock. 1:10. Kicking off her shoes, she stretched out on the sofa. Only seconds later, it seemed, a violent thumping on her door disturbed her.

Miranda groaned at the intrusive noise and burrowed deeper into the lumpy cushion, but the incessant pounding followed her. Groggily she sat up and peered at the door. "Go away," she muttered.

"Ms. Sheffield?" Dave's worried voice demanded an answer. The door handle rattled as he tried to get in.

"Oh, for heaven's sake!" Miranda got to her feet. She stalked to the door, unlocked it and swung it open.

The relief on Dave's face made her feel ashamed of her ill humor. It wasn't his fault that he wasn't Robert.

"Sorry to take so long." She gave him a warm smile to make up for her snappishness. "I must have drifted off." She stepped aside to let him in.

"No problem. I'll just go downstairs and check the furnace and then follow your car back to the lodge. Robert got held up with a broken leg."

"Broken leg!" Miranda felt her stomach clench in a sudden spasm of fear. "How'd he do that?"

"Not him. One of the skiers. A rank beginner decided to tackle the experienced slope. He fell halfway down. He's lucky it was a good clean break. Some of 'em are real messy. I won't be a minute." He disappeared down the cellar stairs.

Miranda refused to analyze the fear she'd felt, telling herself instead that even the most modern woman would be worried about the man she was involved with. Hurriedly she slipped into her coat and went to retrieve the overnight case she'd packed earlier.

She navigated the distance to the lodge without problems. She parked her car at the back of the lot and made her way through the crowded lounge. Her gaze swept the room. The sight of a plate of irregularly cut cheese cubes reminded her of her promise to talk to Mrs. Kolcheck. It was not a task she welcomed.

She found Mrs. Kolcheck sitting in the kitchen with her feet propped on a stool and a large mug of coffee in her hand.

"Good afternoon." Miranda gave her a cheerful smile.

"I'm taking my break before the evening rush begins," Mrs. Kolcheck said defensively.

"Mind if I join you?"

"Help yourself." Mrs. Kolcheck heaved a dispirited sigh. "I figured you'd be coming. Mr. Deverill said he gave you some of the desserts I made."

"He did." Miranda slowly poured herself a cup of coffee while she tried to decide the best way to tackle the situation. Head-on, she finally decided. Mrs. Kolcheck would probably miss the point if she tried a subtle approach.

"They weren't much like yours." Mrs. Kolcheck had given her the opening she wanted.

"They weren't anything like mine," Miranda said bluntly, pausing at the stricken look on Mrs. Kolcheck's face. What was going on here? Mrs. Kolcheck certainly wasn't acting like someone who'd intentionally sabotaged the recipes, but it was straining the bounds of credulity to believe that the woman had accidentally messed up both of them.

"Mrs. Kolcheck, neither Mr. Deverill or I can understand how someone who cooks as well as you do couldn't make those recipes I gave you."

"Well...you see..." Mrs. Kolcheck nervously tapped the handle of her coffee mug. "My mother taught me to cook all that other stuff years ago."

"Yes?" Miranda probed, not understanding the connection.

"When Mr. Deverill asked me to make some more of those desserts of yours..." She looked anguished. "I watched you as hard as I could, and I tried my best to remember, but you did all three so fast."

"But I left you copies of . . ." Miranda paused; a suspicion began to grow, and she leaned toward the other woman. "Mrs. Kolcheck, is the problem that you can't read?"

Mrs. Kolcheck's bottom lip trembled, and her faded, blue eyes filled with tears. "Yes," she whispered. "When I was young, I never had much chance to go to school. My ma was sickly most of the time, and I had to help look after my brothers. Then I was too old to be sitting in a beginning class with a bunch of little kids, so I didn't. My pa said that book learning wasn't all that important for a woman, anyhow." She continued nervously. "I can cook things I know. And for things I don't know, my daughter helps me go over the recipes until I have them in my mind, but she was out of town this week." Mrs. Kolcheck looked around the kitchen sadly. "This was such a great job. It paid more than I ever earned before. Lots more. Had insurance, too."

"Still does, as far as I know." Miranda smiled at her warmly.

"Yeah, but once Mr. Deverill finds out that I can't read . . ."

"I guarantee that Mr. Deverill is not going to fire you," Miranda said, knowing it was true. Robert was not only basically a kind man, but also a very practical one. He needed Mrs. Kolcheck.

"But what am I going to do?" she wailed.

"It seems to me that learning to read would be the logical solution," Miranda said.

Mrs. Kolcheck looked dumbfounded. "Learn to read! But I'm fifty-seven years old."

"So? If I were suggesting you learn skydiving, you might have a point, but reading is a mental activity and there's nothing wrong with your mind."

"You think I could learn?" Mrs. Kolcheck asked wistfully. "I'd sure like to be able to read to my grandkids."

"Absolutely," Miranda said with total conviction. "Why don't you call the library and ask them if they have a tutoring program? In the meantime I'll record those recipes on tape, and you can play them back whenever you need to make them."

"Thank you." Mrs. Kolcheck gave her a beaming smile. "You're just as nice inside as you are outside. I'm so glad you're going to marry our Mr. Deverill."

"Marry Mr. Deverill?" Miranda repeated, caught unawares by the longing that flooded her at the thought.

"You'd be perfect. You're beautiful and he's handsome and he's got the inn and you bake and he wants to expand and you got the farm."

The mention of the farm brought Miranda back to earth with a thump. "I have a friend I'll introduce you to someday. She views marriage the same way you do."

"Practical reasons are the best for marrying," Mrs. Kolcheck insisted. "Sex is well and good, but it don't last."

Miranda winced. In the case of her first marriage, it hadn't even begun. She simply hadn't had enough experience to know what had been missing. But now she did, and she couldn't believe that what she felt for Robert was going to fade. In fact, it seemed to be growing stronger.

She got to her feet, eager to end the unsettling conversation. "I'll keep your advice in mind if he should show any interest."

"Oh, he's interested, all right," Mrs. Kolcheck assured her. "His eyes are different when they look at you. They kind of sparkle. Everyone's noticed it. He never looked like that when any of his other girlfriends visited."

"Other girlfriends?" Miranda hated asking the question, but couldn't help herself. She had to know if he was involved with anyone else.

"Maud says that when the lodge first opened up a couple years back, he had lots of women friends to stay, but that nothing ever came of it. They were just friends, if you know what I mean."

A brief image of her ex-husband floated across Miranda's mind and she nodded. "I know exactly what you mean."

10

MIRANDA PEERED through the open door of Robert's office. Her heart skipped a beat when she saw his dark head bent over his desk. Compulsively she examined the breadth of his shoulders, lingering on the muscles outlined beneath the yellow cashmere sweater. He looked like a very marriageable man, she conceded. In fact, he'd probably bring new meaning to the institution of marriage.

"Ah." He gave her a smile that lifted the corners of his mouth as well as her spirits. "I thought I felt a disturbance in the air. Come in."

Miranda did, closing the door behind her. She intended to kiss him and didn't want an audience.

"How do you feel?" He studied her critically. "Let me see your wrist."

Miranda obligingly held it out.

"It looks . . . angry," he finally said.

"You'd look angry, too, if someone sliced you open," she answered absently, her attention focused on the way his hair grew at the nape of his neck.

"That's not what I meant. What did you do today?"

"Dave had to wake me up from a nap when he came," she replied, giving him part of the truth.

"Yes, but what were you doing in between the time I left and the time Dave woke you up?" Reaching out, he grabbed her good arm and gently pulled her onto his lap. He cradled her against his chest with his left arm while his right hand slipped beneath her sweater to lie upon the gentle swell of her breasts. His callused palm felt warm, abrasive and exciting against her skin. Miranda snuggled closer.

"I—" she began.

"Shh. I'm counting."

She tilted her head and stared at his absorbed expression. "Counting what?"

"Your pulse rate."

Miranda considered his answer. "I think pulses are measured at the wrist," she finally said.

"You measure your way. I'll measure mine. I'm not getting a very good reading. It's skittering all over the place." Moving lower, the tips of his fingers slipped beneath her lacy bra.

Miranda tensed as his hand suddenly penetrated further, cupping one small breast. She heard her breath whistle between her parted lips and felt her whole body quicken. It no longer mattered that they were in an office with a minimal amount of privacy. Nothing mattered but the reality of Robert and the demands of her body.

She twisted slightly in order to fit herself more closely against him. Clearly every bit as eager as she was, his mouth covered hers and his tongue surged inside. She met it, engaging in a duel of desire that left her body trembling. She wanted more, much more than simply kissing him. She wanted—

The brisk rap upon the door was an unbearable intrusion. Robert lifted his head. "Dammit!" His curse echoed Miranda's sentiments exactly. "Just a minute!"

Not wanting to give rise to even more gossip, Miranda hastily slipped off his lap and, pushing aside several stacks of paper, perched on the edge of his oversize desk.

Robert eyed her in frustration. It seemed as if every time he finally got her into his arms, something interrupted them. Spending time in this damn place was worse than living in a fishbowl, and in hers was nothing more than glorified indoor camping. His mood—sharp frustration—softened miraculously when he noticed the faint tremor in her fingers as she played with his cloisonné paperweight. The knowledge that Miranda felt the way he did calmed him. Tonight, he promised himself. Just as soon as he could get her alone with a reasonable chance of being uninterrupted, he'd make mad, passionate love to her.

The rapping started again. "Come in," he called.

"Robert, I'm sorry, but I forgot to tell you when you got back that Axel called."

Robert felt Miranda tense at the name and decided that this might be the time to risk bringing up the matter of the missing art.

"Thanks, Maud. I'll call him later." He waited until Maud had left, then said casually, "Axel probably just wants to fill me in on his latest find. His hobby is tracking down missing art."

"Missing art?" Miranda tried her best to sound no more than vaguely interested.

"You'd be surprised how much of it was pilfered after the Second World War. A lot of otherwise moral people thought that because they were taking something from an institution instead of an individual, they weren't really doing anything wrong. Kind of like thinking it's all right to cheat on your income taxes."

"I would imagine your cousin soon disabuses them of that notion," Miranda said wryly.

"Yes." Robert bit back renewed frustration. Why wouldn't she confide in him? She was not a greedy person. Everything he'd learned about her told him that.

He tried a different tack. "Not only that, but trying to dispose of stolen art is nothing but trouble."

Stolen art was nothing but trouble, period. Never mind whether you were trying to dispose of, hang on to, or just find it. She'd been right not to tell him about the paintings, she thought grimly. Given his unyielding attitude toward theft and with his cousin lobbying for a search warrant, Robert would never help her hush the whole mess up.

Desperately seeking an innocuous subject, her eyes alighted upon the stack of papers on his desk. "What are all those?" she asked.

Deciding he'd said enough for now, he allowed her to change the subject. "Government forms. When I first took over the lodge, I used to have nightmares that I was drowning in a sea of paperwork."

"Are there that many government forms?"

"State, local and federal income taxes, sales taxes, property taxes, inventory taxes, liquor taxes, forms for the employees' pensions, bonuses, forms from the liquor commission, the health department . . . The list seems endless at times." He grimaced. "Actually, the list seems endless all the time."

"Can't you hire someone to do it?" Miranda asked.

"I do, but I have to go over everything, because it's my name on the bottom line, and if there's a mistake, it's my responsibility."

"I see." Felker and Felker had at least as many employees as the lodge, maybe more. She'd known, of course, that there'd be paperwork involved with the ordering of supplies and the like, but had never really considered the sheer volume of government forms to be handled. She swallowed uneasily. If she insisted on being the one to buy Jim out, then all those forms would become her responsibility.

"What are you thinking about?" Robert asked.

She sighed. "The hard facts of life out there in the working world. By the way—" Miranda suddenly remembered the cook "—I solved your problem with Mrs. Kolcheck's desserts."

"Good. What exactly was my problem, by the way?"

"She couldn't recreate my recipes because she couldn't read them."

"She what?" Robert stared at Miranda in astonishment. "But she signed all kinds of forms when I hired her."

Miranda shrugged. "I didn't say that she couldn't write her name. I said she couldn't read. She's going to look into an adult reading program. In the meantime, I'm going to make tapes of my recipes for her. And speaking of recipes, I'll think I'll go cook dinner for us while you finish up here."

"Rest instead. We can order from room service. I always do."

She eyed him thoughtfully. "When was the last time you had your cholesterol level checked?"

"Last fall. It was 162," he said smugly.

"There's no reason to look so pleased with yourself. Considering what you eat, if your count's that low, it's because you've got good genes."

"And I work them out in the basement every day," he said, defending himself. "Exercise is important to good health."

"Basement?" she asked, her interest caught.

"That's where the gym is. There's a weight room, racquetball courts, a spa, that kind of stuff."

"Ah, yes." She gave him a saccharine smile. "I remember. That's the place where you're going to put your bar. I'll have to check it out after I cook dinner." She headed toward the door.

"Stay out of the basement until after your arm is healed. And don't overdo the cooking," he called after her.

By the time dinner was over, Miranda was beginning to wish she'd listened to him and let him order their meal from room service. Not only was she exhausted, but some of the muscles she'd used earlier in prying up the floorboards were beginning to ache. After putting away the last of the now-clean pots in the suite's tiny kitchen, she poured two mugs of coffee and carried them into the living room, where Robert was adding logs to the crackling fire.

She set the cups upon the raised hearth, then tried wriggling her sore shoulders, but it didn't help.

"Are you sore?" Robert asked.

"Not much." She shrugged, then winced when her shoulders protested the movement.

Robert frowned. "I don't understand why your shoulders would be sore when it was your wrist that was hurt."

"It must be that I changed the way I normally move to accommodate my cut." She gave him an innocent look.

"What you need is a massage."

"Massage?" Her eyes roamed speculatively over his well-muscled shoulders and down his arms to linger on his hands. A shiver of awareness slithered through her at the memory of his fingers on her skin, touching, stroking. "What do you know about massages?"

"Quite a bit, actually." He picked up an afghan that lay at the end of the couch and spread it upon the floor in front of the fire. "Massages need a firm surface," he told her. "Now strip off your sweater and lie down."

"Strip off . . . ?" Her voice cracked.

"I can hardly give you a massage through your sweater, now can I?" he asked with a reasonableness belied by the gleam dancing in his hazel eyes.

Miranda felt a lurch of excitement; he wasn't anywhere as detached as she'd first thought.

Being careful with her arm, Miranda quickly wriggled out of her sweater and tossed it onto the couch. The cool air rushed over her heated skin, making her shiver.

The gleam in his eye intensified as he studied her small breasts, which were barely covered by the satin bra she was wearing. "Miranda Sheffield, you are an incredibly beautiful woman. But I digress," he added on a brisker note.

"So digress a little," she murmured with her best come-hither look. To her intense satisfaction the glow in his eyes intensified, taking on a greenish sheen.

"Business before pleasure." He seemed to be making a monumental effort to rein in his emotions.

"Promises, promises." Miranda smiled seductively as excitement raged through her. She was willing to put up with any amount of pummeling if the reward was making love with Robert.

"Down, woman." He pointed to the afghan.

"Now there's a phrase full of Freudian implications," she muttered, trying to find a comfortable position on the floor. She couldn't.

Robert dropped to his knees beside her and lightly touched a spot just above the waistband of her slacks. "What caused these strange little bluish bruises?"

"I don't know," she lied, knowing they must have happened when the crowbar slipped and hit her. With painful repetitiveness. But she could hardly tell him that. Miranda swallowed a sigh. She was becoming very tired of having to watch what she said to him. On the contrary, she felt an increasing compulsion to share everything with him. Her hopes, her uncertainty, her problems... Especially her problems. But she couldn't; the biggest one wasn't her problem alone.

Dammit all, anyway. Robert silently cursed her reticence. What had she been doing to get those bruises? There were too many of them for her to have simply

tripped over something. Although . . . He shook his
head in puzzlement. Could she have climbed into the
loft, then fallen out? Was that why she wouldn't tell him
what had happened? Because she'd broken her word
while looking for that damned art? He was frustrated.
He wanted to protect her, to keep her safe, but he
couldn't.

But for the moment, at least, she was safe here with
him. He flexed his fingers and placed them upon her
shoulders. Trying to blank out the feel of her supple
skin beneath his fingertips, Robert began to methodi-
cally knead the muscles in her shoulders. It wasn't an
easy task. A faint scent of flowers rose from her body
as he worked and played havoc with his concentration.

Miranda gasped as his fingers slowly began to stroke
down the side of her neck. A shivery sensation quiv-
ered to life, fueled not only by the insidious magic of
his hands but by the memory of their previous lovemaking. She knew what was going to happen and was
finding it hard to wait.

Taking a deep breath, she rolled over and stared into
Robert's face. It was a series of planes and angles and
his lips were pressed together as if he were under enor-
mous strain.

Miranda reached up and traced his jawline, reveling
in the raspy texture of his skin. Physically he was so

different from her, yet they fitted together perfectly. Two halves of the same whole.

Robert pushed his fingers through her curls and began to rub circles on her temple with his thumbs. She felt like purring. "Mmm, that feels so good," she murmured.

"I aim to please."

Miranda pursed her lips as if considering his words. "Well, if you aim to please, I have a complaint."

"How so?"

"You have too many clothes on." Anticipation made her breathless.

"Yes." He nodded solemnly. "I can see how a lady without a sweater might feel that way. What'll you trade me for it?"

The pupils in his eyes expanded, and Miranda watched in fascination. "Trade?" The word came out on a husky sigh.

"Sure. Everything in the world's a trade-off. So what are you offering for my shirt?"

"What do you want?"

"Let me think." He appeared to be giving the matter serious consideration. "Tell you what, since I'm not wearing an undershirt, I'll trade you my shirt for your bra."

Miranda felt a bright curl of excitement slither through her. "It's a deal," she said. "You go first." She looked on, bewitched, while his long fingers hastily unbuttoned his shirt. He shrugged out of it to reveal a broad expanse of hair-roughened chest. Carelessly tossing the shirt behind him, he eyed her expectantly.

Miranda swallowed her sudden nervousness. Somehow, taking off her clothes with Robert watching her seemed much more intimate than doing it when they were making love.

She fumbled with her bra clasp and, finally freeing it, tossed it after his shirt with what she hoped was a sophisticated gesture. Inside, she certainly didn't feel sophisticated. She felt trembly and unsure of herself. Despite having been married for the better part of ten years, she felt as if she were just beginning to understand what physical love between a man and a woman was all about.

"You remind me of a statue of a nymph I once saw in Crete." Robert's husky voice scraped over her nerve endings. "Perfectly shaped and infinitely graceful. Only unlike the marble image, you're real. Real and touchable." A wicked grin lifted his lips. "What will you trade me for my jeans?"

It took a second for his question to sink in.

"Mmm. An even trade. My slacks for your jeans."

"Done." He shoved the zipper down and stepped out of them, kicking them to one side. Miranda swallowed hard at the sight of his penis straining against his white cotton briefs. Not taking her eyes off the evidence of his desire, she pushed her slacks over her slim hips and wriggled out of them.

Slowly, as if savoring the moment, he put his arms around her. Sighing with pleasure—things could only get better—she laid her head upon his shoulder. The faintly musky scent of his cologne drifted into her lungs and she buried her face against his neck to intensify the aromatic experience.

She could feel his heart slamming into her chest and it filled her with satisfaction. Her hands drifted over his back, pausing to explore the indentations of his spine.

"I love the feel of you," she murmured. "Like warm silk over coiled steel."

Robert cupped her hips and lifted her against him. His head swooped down to lick the pebbly-hard tip of one of her breasts.

"Robert!" Miranda clutched his shoulders, trying to find an anchor against the tide of emotion buffeting her.

He sank to his knees with her still in his arms, then rolled onto the afghan.

His hand stroked over her breasts with a feather-light gesture that excited her unbearably. She could feel them swelling, tautening under the impact of his caress and uttered an inarticulate cry.

"What is it you want, my darling?" he whispered against the fluttering pulse at the base of her throat.

"You." She pressed frantic little kisses upon his chest.

Robert continued his stroking, moving downward over the silky material of her panties. Miranda gasped and felt her skin flutter beneath his fingertips. An ache deep inside her cried out for him.

"Robert," she moaned.

He yanked off first his shorts and then her panties with a rough impatience that found an answering echo deep within her. Once again she grasped his shoulders and tried to pull him closer.

Bracing himself on his arms, he rolled on top of her and using one knee, parted her slender thighs. Just for a second the weight of his body was sufficient, then it wasn't. She wanted more. Much more. She dug her heels into the soft afghan and pushed upward against him.

"Patience, my precious." Robert framed her face with his hands. His mouth rubbed lightly back and forth upon hers, then finally captured her lips. His tongue surged inside to explore.

Before her initial burst of excitement could fade, he pushed his hips forward with one powerful thrust, filling her. Her heart was beating so hard it seemed to block her throat.

Frantic now, she wrapped her legs around his waist in an attempt to get even closer.

"Yes and yes and yes." He accompanied each word with a powerful thrust of his hips, and finally snapped the fragile cord tethering her to reality.

"BUT WHY won't you move in with me?" Robert repeated the question for what seemed like the thousandth time. The problem wasn't so much his insistence as her own intense desire to do just that, she admitted honestly. The depth of her longing scared her. She felt as if she were getting in too deeply, too fast. She needed some time to put her mushrooming feelings for Robert into perspective. Time and space. And looming over the problem of her chaotic emotions was the even bigger one of the paintings. She stared blindly out the truck's windshield. The ever-present problem of the paintings.

She clutched the door handle of his truck as he steered it around her barn. "I have to come back here during the day," she repeated doggedly.

"Hasn't anyone ever told you that stubbornness is an unattractive trait?" he inquired in frustration, knowing full well why she'd insisted on returning. Somehow he had to find that art and find it soon, so that it no longer stood between them. Then he could try to move their relationship forward. Each day seemed to drive home the conclusion that they were perfectly matched. Their careers meshed, so did their interests, and sexually, things simply didn't get any better.

If he could just figure out why she was so determined to get her hands on that art, then he stood a chance of talking her out of it.

"Thank you." She grinned at him.

Robert stared at her blankly. "For what?" he finally asked.

"For not saying that stubbornness in a woman is an unattractive trait."

"Not a chance." He grinned back. "I don't have a masochistic bone in my body. And don't you dare come back tonight with another set of bruises."

"I'll try for a different set," she said, knowing full well that the first thing she was going to do was head for the attic and continue ripping up floorboards. She felt as if her entire life was on hold until she could locate those blasted paintings.

She pushed the door open. "Thanks for the ride."

"Thank me later." He got out of the truck with her. "After I've made sure it's safe."

Safe? Safe from what? she wondered. The only other person with any interest in the contents of the house was the autocratic Axel, and he was in Germany.

He waited until she unlocked the front door, then preceded her in. It took him five minutes to check all the rooms.

"All clear." He emerged from the bedroom. "You ought to take a nap."

"I've only been up a couple of hours and, besides, I feel great. My arm is only marginally sore."

"Promise me you'll take it easy."

"I promise I won't do anything foolhardy," she temporized.

"I suppose I'll have to be happy with that." He paused by the front door. "You mentioned thanking me?"

"What did you have in mind?" Her eyes went to his firm lips.

"What I always seem to have in mind around you."

Miranda laughed lightheartedly. "You, sir, are insatiable." She reached up and kissed him. "There, that should hold you till later."

"I'd like to hold you till later," he grumbled as he left.

Miranda stood in front of the living-room window and watched until Robert's car had disappeared into the stand of pines between the farm and the lodge. She sighed and turned away. The sooner she found those paintings, the sooner she could escape from what seemed like solitary confinement and spend her days at the lodge amid the hustle and bustle of people. This evening she'd be part of it, she determined, firming her sagging resolve. Maybe this time she'd have better luck. Superstitious, she crossed her fingers.

It didn't help. By four o'clock, she had pried up every third floorboard in the entire attic and found nothing for her troubles but dead mice, the skeleton of a squirrel and various bits and pieces that she felt best not to examine too closely.

Finally admitting defeat, she carefully skirted the boxes and trunks she had stacked chest high and went downstairs to run herself a bath. There was no reason for her to stay at the farm any longer today. The sooner she got the dust and dirt from the attic removed, the quicker she could go back to the lodge. And Robert.

11

MIRANDA WAITED by the reception desk until Maud had finished with the couple checking in, then asked, "Maud, do you know where—? Oh, never mind." She saw Robert emerge from the ski shop.

He smiled intimately as he caught sight of her and, taking her arm, hurried her down the corridor to his suite, pretending not to hear the tall man who hailed him. Unlocking his door, he gestured her inside, closing the door behind them with a snap.

"The minute the snow thaws, I'm digging," he said emphatically.

"Digging?" Miranda blinked uncertainly. Her uncle couldn't have buried the paintings, could he?

"For a house," Robert elaborated. "The constant interruptions around this place have always annoyed me, but since I met you, they've become intolerable."

She grimaced. "I know exactly what you mean. What we need—" She was interrupted by the phone.

"Is some privacy," Robert muttered, grabbed the phone and barked out a curt, "What? Who did you say?"

He partially turned and studied her, as if trying to make up his mind about something. "It's for you," he finally said. "Your ex-husband. He says he has to talk to you."

"Jim?" Miranda probed her reaction and was surprised to discover all she felt was annoyance at the untimely interruption.

Robert broke into her thoughts. "Do you want to talk to him?"

"Not particularly. I'd much rather kiss you," she admitted candidly. "Although I am curious to know how he knew I was here."

"He says when he couldn't get you at the farm, he called your mother in Belgium and she suggested he try here." Robert handed her the receiver.

Miranda gingerly held it to her ear. "Yes?"

"Miranda, this . . . um . . . is Jim."

"I recognize your voice," she said dryly.

"Mmm, Brandy and I talked it over with our lawyer, and we have an alternative offer, which I think is very generous of us, considering the fact that Brandy is pregnant."

"Pregnancy precludes generosity?" she asked. What she really wanted to know was how Brandy could be pregnant if Jim was sterile. She reined in her curiosity. No. She didn't want to know. It was none of her business.

"We shall have an heir to consider, which is why I feel we're being very generous with our offer," he said ponderously.

Miranda tried to hurry him up. "Which is?"

"Since your lawyer claims that a good part of the success of the business is due to your reputation as a pastry chef rather than my talent as a business manager, he proposes the following. The business will be valued, and I'll pay you one half the cash value up front. Then I'll pay you ten percent of the business's net profit next year, nine percent the year after that, eight the next year and so on until the tenth year. Then I'll pay you one percent and the business is all mine."

"An interesting proposition," she murmured. "Very well. I accept." She felt a tremendous sense of relief.

"You mean it?" His voice rose excitedly.

"Yes. You can work out the details with my lawyer. Goodbye." She hung up on his volatile thanks.

"A problem?" Robert asked, wanting to probe her reaction to her ex-husband's call, but not wanting to upset her.

"No," she said slowly, savoring a sense of freedom. "I merely decided that what I liked about the catering business was the baking, not all that paperwork that Jim seems to revel in. So he can have it."

"And the baby?" Her openness encouraged him to continue.

"The baby?" She weighed her reaction to Jim's news. She felt very little, really, except a faint sense of envy. A baby would be nice, but not just any baby. She wanted Robert's baby, because she loved him. Miranda felt her eyes widen with something akin to horror at the unexpected bit of self-discovery. She couldn't be in love with him! Agitated, she rubbed her forehead.

She was merely having a very modern affair with a man she liked a lot. The problem was that she wasn't all that modern in her thinking, and somewhere along the line, without her even noticing it, her liking had slipped into loving.

Oh, Miranda, that was definitely not one of your brighter moves, she thought grimly.

"You do mind," Robert said.

"No! I don't! Truly." She clutched his arm. It was of vital importance that she convince him. The situation was complicated enough without Robert thinking that she was pining for her ex-husband. She focused on an excuse she thought he'd understand. "It's just that it's a bit of a wrench, saying I'll sell the business. I know it's the right decision, but it's still a bit scary to be cut adrift, so to speak."

"You aren't adrift." He pulled her into his arms. "You're anchored very firmly, right here." He lowered his head to kiss her, then froze when the phone rang again.

"On second thought, I may not wait for the spring thaw," he said. "I may simply cut the snow into blocks and build us an igloo." He picked up the phone. "Yes?" he asked in resignation. "What?" His voice changed, becoming concerned. "That's right. Have Dave get the ambulance sled out. I'll be there in a minute."

"What's wrong?" Miranda asked the minute he hung up.

"A couple of teenage boys from town snuck onto the slopes and one of them fell and can't get up, according to his friend who just staggered in."

"Staggered? Was he hurt, too?"

"No. He's simply nine-tenths drunk." Robert grimaced and hurriedly slipped into his jacket. He gave her a brief, hard kiss. "Save my place. I'll be back just as soon as I can." He pulled his hat and gloves out of his pocket and left.

Miranda sank onto the sofa, knowing it could be hours before he returned. She stared at the tiny golden flecks of color in the ceiling and tried to think. She wasn't at all sure she wanted to be in love. There wasn't a great deal of emotional security for a woman in love. In fact, from what she could see, there wasn't any at all. She didn't even know if Robert returned her love.

Even if Robert didn't love her, he definitely liked her, respected her as a person and admired her competence as a chef. On the other hand, he not only wanted to get his hands on her farm, but was hot on the trail of her stolen paintings. How much were those two facts coloring his reaction?

Exactly what do you want from Robert? she asked herself. She stared at the fireplace as if she might find the answer in the crackling flames.

"I want to marry him." She spoke the words slowly, as if trying them on for size, then repeated them more firmly when she discovered they were a perfect fit. She wanted to marry Robert Deverill and run his kitchens while he ran the lodge itself. It was an ideal match in every way. Not only did she love him to distraction, but their careers meshed perfectly. She could make a very real contribution to the smooth running of the inn and gain a great deal of personal satisfaction in doing so.

And if the fates were kind, they might one day have children. A smile curved her lips at the thought of holding their baby in her arms.

Her smile faded; she remembered the stolen paintings. The urge to confide in him was almost overwhelming, but she couldn't. She just couldn't. There was too much at stake, and if she was wrong . . . She'd been wrong about a man before. Doubts began to creep in. Not only had she been wrong about Jim's feelings toward her, but she hadn't even noticed when he'd cheated on her.

Because she hadn't cared enough to take a good look at all his half-hearted excuses, she suddenly realized. She simply hadn't cared where he'd been spending his evenings. She never would have been that sanguine about Robert.

There was nothing wrong with her judgment, she told herself. What had been wrong had been her own cowardly refusal to face the fact that their marriage was dead and needed a decent burial. Jim had never done more than merely scratch the surface of her emotions. Robert had thrown them into absolute turmoil the minute they'd met.

So where did she go from here? Her best bet was probably to play a waiting game while she intensified her search for the paintings, she decided. Once she had them safely returned, then she could move in with Robert as he wanted her to. In the meantime, she'd surround him with so much love that he wouldn't have any choice but to fall in love with her.

ROBERT STUCK HIS HEAD around the kitchen door, brightening when he saw Miranda standing beside Mrs. Kolcheck at the stove.

"Ah, there you are," he said.

"Good morning." Miranda walked toward him, her obvious pleasure at seeing him adding a sparkle to her eyes. "I looked for you when I arrived half an hour ago, but you weren't in your office or the suite."

He grasped the back of her neck and pulled her forward for a quick, hard kiss. "If you'd just move in, you'd know where I was."

I sure would. Miranda sighed ruefully. He'd be over at the farmhouse, searching for the paintings. If only she knew how long it took to get a search warrant issued. Or even if he could get one with the amount of evidence he had. She felt as if she were sitting on a time bomb that might go off at any minute.

"I'm sorry." Robert must have misunderstood her sigh. "I promise not to nag. At least, not anymore today." He gave her a tender smile that made her feel cherished. "It's just that I want you around all the time. Not just in bed at night."

"Shh." Miranda cast a furtive glance around the busy kitchen. No one appeared to have overheard him.

Robert snorted. "You think they don't know what's going on? This place is a hotbed of gossip."

"Don't you mind?" Miranda asked curiously.

"As far as I'm concerned, the whole world can know that I think you're the most fascinating woman I've ever met."

Then why doesn't he suggest marriage? Miranda wondered in frustration. *Why doesn't he suggest making my presence permanent? Why don't you?* she mocked herself. There was no law that said a woman couldn't propose. But if she pushed him and he wasn't ready for a commitment, it would destroy what they did have. He'd back off, and pretty soon they'd be polite strangers, uncomfortable with what they'd once shared. No, she decided, it was far better to play a waiting game, even if it was much harder.

She noticed he was wearing his coat. "Where are you off to?"

"We have to go into town to pick up some stock for the ski shop that just arrived. I came to see if you needed anything."

"No, I'm fine. What time will you be back?"

"About one. Let's have a late lunch in my suite."

"Love to," Miranda murmured, knowing that food would be the last thing they shared.

"Fifty-five minutes on this carrot cake, right?" Mrs. Kolcheck called from the stove, effectively destroying their sense of isolation.

"That's right."

Dave stuck his head around the door. "Robert, the truck's parked out front."

"Coming." With a last quick kiss for Miranda, Robert left.

Miranda slowly turned back to her baking. At least she didn't have to worry about the paintings for a while. He could hardly search for them while Dave was with him.

Forty minutes later, she had finished the baking she'd wanted to do and was about to tape the recipes for Mrs. Kolcheck, when she realized she'd left her recorder back at home.

She glanced around the kitchen, which was becoming busy with the early lunches. This would be a good time to go get it, she decided. The half-mile walk to the farmhouse would invigorate her after a morning spent inside.

Miranda bundled up warmly and stepped outside. The temperature was in the mid-twenties, which felt like a heat wave, considering what it had been. Taking a deep breath, she started off at a brisk pace, enjoying the warm feel of the sun against her skin.

Ten minutes later she reached the farmhouse. She started to unlock the door, frowning when she realized it wasn't locked. She pulled her cap off her head and quietly stepped inside, listening. She knew she'd locked that door before she'd left this morning. After ten years of living in New York City, it was second nature for her to lock up.

Could Robert be here looking for the paintings? she wondered, then dismissed the idea. He'd left in the truck with Dave. He couldn't have returned early because the truck wasn't here. Whoever had jimmied the ancient lock on that door had come on foot. Hopefully come and gone.

Miranda carefully took the rifle from the rack by the door and slipping off her boots, crept toward the bedroom. A thump from the attic overhead made her freeze, and she tightened her grip on the rifle. She gazed longingly at the phone, wishing she could simply call the sheriff and let him deal with the intruder, but she didn't dare. Whoever was up there might know something about the paintings.

Miranda drew a shaky breath and tried to think. The problem was she didn't know enough to make any plans. The only thing she knew for certain was that she had to scare off whoever was up there.

Taking a deep breath, she gathered her courage and crept across the floor to the attic stairs. There was the distinct sound of something being dragged across the floor.

She paused halfway up to pinpoint the intruder's location. Once she was sure there was only one and he was to the right of the stairwell, she bounded up the last steps in a rush and, pointing the rifle in the direction of the noise, yelled, "Freeze, or I'll fill you full of lead!"

"What the hell?" Robert swung around at the sound of her voice, stepped on one of the boards she'd pried loose earlier and lost his balance, falling against the stack of trunks behind him, knocking them over.

Miranda winced. "Robert! You scared me out of my wits."

"I scared you! You're the one who came charging up the stairs like something out of *Gang Busters*, waving a deadly weapon." He pushed aside one of the trunks he'd knocked over and got to his feet. "That gun has got to go. It—" His sudden stillness sent a chill of foreboding over Miranda. Had he hurt himself when he'd fallen?

"Robert, what—?" She moved toward him, only to come to a precipitous halt when she realized what he was looking at. The fall had loosened the—obviously false—bottom of one of the trunks, spilling its contents onto the attic floor.

Miranda sucked her breath in; the sun streaming through the window illuminated the flesh tones of the plump nude in the painting. A sense of awe gripped her at its exquisite perfection.

"So Axel was right." Robert reached out.

"Leave them alone," Miranda ordered, trying to think.

"How do you intend to stop me?" he asked. "With that?" He gestured toward the rifle.

Miranda looked down, surprised to see the rifle still in her hands. "Of course not. I would never hurt you." She carefully set the gun down.

She felt like sitting in the middle of the floor and crying. After all the work she'd put into finding those blasted paintings, they'd been in the attic all the time. A false bottom on a trunk had never even occurred to her.

Miserable, she looked at Robert; the six feet separating them yawned like an uncrossable chasm.

"Those paintings belong to the German people. I'm not going to let you keep them," he said slowly, trying to gauge her reaction.

"I don't want to," she snapped, hurt that he could even think that she would.

"Then why didn't you tell me? We could have looked together."

"Because you were so self-righteous about stealing from museums that I figured you'd never help me hush the whole mess up. And even if you were willing," she rushed on when he opened his mouth again, "there was Axel. I saw that letter he sent."

"What you didn't see was my response. I asked him to hold off for a while while I tried to handle things myself."

"I still don't trust Axel. He'll take the pictures back and tell everyone that Uncle Henry stole them."

"Henry's dead," Robert pointed out.

"It isn't Henry I'm worried about. It's my stepfather."

"He's after the paintings, too?"

"He doesn't even know about the paintings. He's to be the new U.S. ambassador to Germany."

Robert whistled softly. "I see. That does rather complicate matters."

Miranda grimaced. "To put it mildly. All I want to do is mail these things to the German Embassy in Washington."

Robert shook his head. "Bad idea."

"But..."

"First of all, you should never send anything irreplaceable through the mails. Secondly, suppose the embassy clerk who opens the package decides to keep them."

Miranda ran trembling fingers through her hair as the truth of what he was saying registered.

"Listen to me, Miranda," Robert said urgently. "Axel and I simply want the paintings safely restored. We don't care about publicity."

"But Axel..."

"Can arrange for the paintings to be returned to the museum where they belong, without anyone being the wiser."

"My stepfather's career..."

"Miranda, I love you," Robert said flatly. "I would never lie to you. I promise you. No one will ever know where they came from."

Miranda heard his words echo eerily through her mind. She wanted desperately to believe them. But overshadowing them was her love for her mother. If she was wrong about Robert... She shuddered at the thought of the inevitable consequences.

Robert watched her agonize for a long moment, then said, "Miranda, trust has to start somewhere. I've told you the truth, and I trust you to make the right decision about those paintings." He walked toward the stairs.

Miranda glanced at the paintings still lying on the floor, then back to him. "Where are you going?" she asked fearfully.

"To the lodge. I meant what I said. Trust has to start somewhere. It would seem that it's going to have to start with me."

"And if I don't give them to you?" she asked through lips that felt numb.

He eyed her silently and said, "I'll be very disappointed, but it won't make any difference to how I feel about you, Miranda. My love for you isn't conditional, based on your doing what I want. Or even on what's right."

"Why did you wait until now to tell me how you feel?" she demanded suspiciously.

He sighed. "Because I thought I was giving you time to come to terms with your feelings for your ex-husband."

"I don't have any feelings for my ex-husband," she said.

He gave her a strained smile. "I know that. But I wasn't sure you did. Think about what I said." He disappeared down the stairs.

Miranda listened to the sound of his footsteps crossing the living room, then heard the clank of her front door closing.

She sank onto a trunk and stared at the accursed paintings as she tried to sort out her chaotic emotions.

One fact stood out. Robert had said he loved her and, if he'd said it, he meant it. Joy momentarily displaced her uncertainty. There was no reason for him to lie in the hope that she'd give him the paintings. He was a lot stronger than she was. He could have simply taken them.

But he hadn't. Gingerly she leaned over and picked them up, carefully laying them out on top of several boxes. There were six of them, ranging from the incomparable Rubens nude to a small one, no more than six by nine inches, of a dead rabbit dripping blood.

Why hadn't he taken them? She chewed her lip in frustration. What was it he'd said? *Trust has to start somewhere?*

She released her breath on a long, whooshing sigh. But it wasn't that simple. If she trusted him and was wrong, then her stepfather's diplomatic career was over. But if she didn't trust him, what was her love worth? Not much, she admitted. If she didn't trust Robert, then there was no foundation for their love to grow on. There would be nothing but sex, and powerful as their physical relationship was, it still needed an anchor. That anchor was trust. If she couldn't trust him, then she didn't love him. Not in any way that mattered.

She stood up, feeling a sense of peace. She loved Robert with all her heart and therefore she trusted him.

Having made up her mind, she was eager to get the paintings to Robert. She took a good-sized cardboard box and carelessly upending its contents onto the floor, packed the paintings in it, using old clothes to wrap them.

Hampered by the awkward size of the box, it took her almost half an hour to walk back to the lodge. Not wanting to field questions from the kitchen staff, she skirted the building and entered through the lobby.

Maud, busy with someone at the desk, didn't even notice Miranda slip past her. Quietly she pushed open the door to Robert's office and entered.

Robert was sitting motionless behind his desk, staring out the window at the mountains. He looked up when she appeared, his set features giving her no clue to his thoughts.

Swallowing nervously, Miranda closed the door behind her and crossed what seemed like acres of carpeting. She set the box upon his desk, took a deep breath and said, "I'm trusting you to see that these get returned without any publicity."

Robert closed his eyes as if sending up a silent prayer. "Thank you." He got to his feet and rounded the desk. "I won't abuse your trust. Not ever." The words sounded like a vow.

Miranda studied him. His eyes gleamed greenly and a sensual smile curved his lips. She felt the now-familiar surge of excitement race along her nerve endings. It was as if the weight of the world had suddenly dropped off her shoulders.

"Aren't you going to call Axel about the paintings?" she finally asked when he continued to simply stare at her.

"First things first." He reached for her, and she went willingly into his arms, snuggling against his hard chest. "First I'm going to make love to you and second, I'm going to make love to you. And then, depending on how tired we are, we'll call Axel."

He gathered her closer and bent his head, only to be interrupted by a knock on the door.

Miranda sighed in resignation.

"Go away!" Robert shouted. "There's no one here."

"But Robert . . ." Maud's voice was muffled by the closed door.

"Robert was kidnapped by space aliens."

"I don't suppose I could speak to the facsimile they left in his place, could I?" Maud grumbled.

"That model isn't functioning yet. Try later. Like tomorrow."

Miranda giggled with pure happiness.

"This is no laughing matter, woman," Robert said. "First thing tomorrow morning we're going to apply for a marriage license. After that we'll call the architect who remodeled the inn for me and ask him to design us a house. As far away from the lodge as we can get and still be on the property."

"Marriage?" Miranda was still occupied with the first part of his sentence. "You want to marry me?"

"Damn right I want to marry you," he said emphatically. "Isn't that what two people who are madly in love normally do?"

"I'm not sure," she said slowly. "This is the first time it's ever happened to me."

"They do," he insisted. "Besides, we have to consider the children. I'd kind of like a mixed set."

"Sounds perfect." She smiled dreamily.

"Robert . . ." Maud's voice interrupted them again. "I really do need to talk to you."

"We'd better hope the stork really does bring babies, or we'll never have any," Miranda grumbled.

"I'll be out in five minutes!" he yelled.

"I'll give you Uncle Henry's farm as a wedding present," Miranda said. "If we build at the very end of it, we can get almost a mile and a half away from this motley crew. But you know," she said seriously, "you don't have to marry me. I'll sell you Uncle Henry's farm, if you prefer."

"You keep Henry's farm. Just add my name to the deed for a wedding present and I'll add yours to the lodge's. We'll run it as partners. And as for marrying you, I'll never have a moment's peace until I tie you down with every bond I can find. Besides . . ." His eyes began to twinkle. "I told you how hard it is to keep a good cook."

"You're doing pretty well at the moment."

"Not half so well as I intend to," he whispered, a second before his lips met hers.

Rebels & Rogues

**Quade had played by their rules ...
now he was making his own.**

**The Patriot
by Lynn Michaels
Temptation #405, August**

All men are not created equal. Some are rough
around the edges. Tough-minded but
tenderhearted. Incredibly sexy. The tempting
fulfillment of every woman's fantasy.

When it's time to fight for what they believe in, to
win that special woman, our Rebels and Rogues are
heroes at heart. Twelve Rebels and Rogues, one
each month in 1992, only from Harlequin
Temptation. Don't miss the upcoming books by
our fabulous authors, including Ruth Jean Dale,
Janice Kaiser and Kelly Street.

WELCOME TO

The quintessential small town where everyone knows everybody else!

Finally, books that capture the pleasure of tuning in to your favorite TV show!

GREAT READING...GREAT SAVINGS...AND A FABULOUS FREE GIFT!

Each book set in Tyler is a self-contained love story; together, the twelve novels stitch the fabric of the community. The covers honor the old American tradition of quilting; each cover depicts a patch of the large Tyler quilt.

With Tyler you can receive a fabulous gift ABSOLUTELY FREE by collecting proofs-of-purchase found in each Tyler book. And use our special Tyler coupons to save on your next TYLER book purchase.

Join your friends at Tyler for the sixth book, SUNSHINE by Pat Warren, available in August.

When Janice Eber becomes a widow, does her husband's friend David provide more than just friendship?

JAYNE ANN KRENTZ

A two-part epic tale from one of today's most popular romance novelists!

Dreams
Parts One & Two

The warrior died at her feet, his blood running out of the cave entrance and mingling with the waterfall. With his last breath he cursed the woman— told her that her spirit would remain chained in the cave forever until a child was created and born there....

So goes the ancient legend of the Chained Lady and the curse that bound her throughout the ages—until destiny brought Diana Prentice and Colby Savager together under the influence of forces beyond their understanding. Suddenly they were both haunted by dreams that linked past and present, while their waking hours were filled with danger. Only when Colby, Diana's modern-day warrior, learned to love, could those dark forces be vanquished. Only then could Diana set the Chained Lady free....

Back by Popular Demand

Janet Dailey
Americana

Janet Dailey takes you on a romantic tour of
America through fifty favorite Harlequin
Presents novels, each one set in a different
state, and researched by Janet and her husband,
Bill.

A journey of a lifetime. The perfect collectable
series!

August titles **#37 OREGON**
To Tell the Truth

#38 PENNSYLVANIA
The Thawing of Mara
